MW01283638

SERPO

Written by
Jason M. Burns

Art by
Joe Eisma

Colors by
Dustin Evans

Letters by
Nick Deschenes

Cover by
Roger Robinson and Nick Bell

For Devil's Due Publishing

Design
Ed Dukeshire

Production
Sam Wells and Sean Dove

Project Managers
Stephen Christy and Cody DeMatteis

INVISIBLE HAND STUDIOS

For Invisible Hand Studios

Vin Di Bona
Chief Editor

Dan Lux
Chief Editor

Jeff Foster
Co-Chief Editor

Special Thanks
Scott Agostoni
and
The William Morris Agency

SERPO Original Graphic Novel, Volume 1. FIRST PRINTING. July, 2008. Published by Devil's Due Publishing, Inc. Office of publication 3759 N. Ravenswood Ave #230, Chicago, IL 60613. Serpo and its logo are trademarks of Freedom Development, LLC., and are used with permission.

FOREWORD

"First let me introduce myself. My name is 'Anonymous'. I am a retired employee of the U.S. Government. I won't go into any great details about my past, but I was involved in a special program..."

– Anonymous

Those were the opening words of an incremental release of extraordinary information that began in November 2005 and has taken the world of UFOlogy by storm: an account of an incredible, true-life 'Lost In Space' like adventure, having allegedly taken place in the 1960s, in which twelve American astronauts spent thirteen long years as part of an exchange program with an alien race.

The planet they were said to have visited was called *Serpo*. And as the story unfolded, it aroused controversy like few other UFO-related claims ever have. Some of the information was compelling, some seemingly ridiculous. Most UFO researchers declined to publicly become embroiled in the debate, but many confirmed privately that they too had received reports that — astonishing as it was to believe — a US-alien exchange program of some sort had indeed taken place.

Debated heatedly on the internet by a fascinated audience of tens of thousands of enthusiasts and critics alike, *Serpo* attracted attention like few other stories. Having volunteered to build a website to archive the releases verbatim as they were received, I found myself at the center of the storm.

As the plot thickened, it became clear that there was a complex back-story involving the US intelligence community at a very high level, which suddenly gave reason why the basics of this story — that American military scientists had visited an alien planet — should be taken very seriously indeed.

At one point, having been given the name of one of the astronauts who reportedly trained with the exchange team but who never actually went on the mission, I tracked down his street address and, with my partner Kerry Cassidy, paid him a surprise visit.

We had told nobody of our plans and had only discussed it very privately between ourselves. Yet when we turned up at his house, his wife was waiting for us at his garden gate while the man himself watched from his doorway, a safe distance away. We had been tracked the entire way.

Although we left immediately, having handed over a courteous note saying we would welcome a meeting (after which we heard nothing from the man), confirmation of the significance of this later came from a senior CIA operative. He was furious. *"Why were you harassing the Old Man?"*, he wrote... our visit had evidently been reported up and down DIA and CIA lines. Thanks... for your confirmation that this was all very real.

Serpo, the graphic novel, is derived from the almost-impossible-to-believe releases, which I and many others have concluded is based on real events leaked to a small number of people, including myself, by high-level inside sources. If this journey occurred in any way close to that which is dramatized here, those enjoying this adventure may pay their own tribute to a team of deserving unsung American heroes.

Bill Ryan
Original webmaster, www.serpo.org, on which all the original information is archived. (Readers please note that I am no longer connected with the Serpo story; however, the current webmaster may be reached through the contact page of the website. July 2008)

CHAPTER ONE

DENVER, CO
Rocky Mountain Times
PRESENT DAY

COME ON, FRED. THROW ME A BONE ON THIS ONE.

I DON'T KNOW WHAT YOU WANT ME TO SAY, CHARLIE, BUT NO MATTER HOW YOU SLICE IT, I'M NOT GONNA CHANGE MY TUNE HERE.
A CRYPTIC EMAIL IS NOT A LEAD. IF THAT WERE THE CASE, I'D SEND YOU OUT TO GET THE SCOOP ON HELPING THE KING OF SOME OBSCURE THIRD WORLD COUNTRY LAUNDER MONEY OR TO LAND THE EXCLUSIVE ON THE MIRACLE DRUG THAT PROMISES TO INCREASE MY PENIS SIZE... TWO BREAKING NEWS STORIES THAT JUST ARRIVED IN MY INBOX.

THIS ISN'T SPAM! NO, I CAN'T POSITIVELY SAY IT'S LEGIT, BUT WHAT IF IT IS? WHAT IF IT LEADS TO SOMETHING BIG?
ALL I'M ASKING FOR IS TWO DAYS TO CHASE THIS TO ITS SOURCE.. HELL, I'LL EVEN TAKE THEM WITHOUT PAY.
UNIVERSITY
EST. 1971

THE ONLY THING YOU'RE GOING TO BE CHASING IS YOUR OWN ASS.
WELL THAT MEANS I'LL BE THE ONE WITH CRAP ON MY FACE.
FINE! TWO DAYS*!* BUT I WANT YOU BACK HERE FRIDAY NIGHT... AND DON'T RETURN EMPTY HANDED.

BRING ME A STORY I CAN PRINT, OR SO HELP ME, I'LL MAKE SURE YOU'RE COVERING TOWN MEETINGS FOR THE NEXT YEAR.

CHRIST! I THOUGHT TOWNS LIKE THIS ONLY EXISTED IN BAD MOVIES!
HEY, OLD TIMER... YOU WOULDN'T BY CHANCE KNOW WHERE I COULD FIND THE SUNSET DINER, WOULD YOU?
NOT AROUND HERE, THAT'S FOR SURE.
WELL, I WAS TOLD IT WAS ON MAIN STREET, DOES THAT SOUND ABOUT RIGHT?

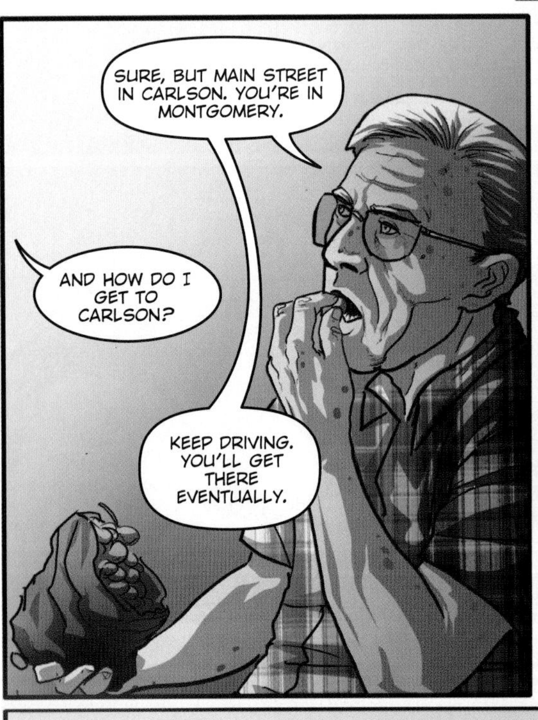
SURE, BUT MAIN STREET IN CARLSON. YOU'RE IN MONTGOMERY.
AND HOW DO I GET TO CARLSON?
KEEP DRIVING. YOU'LL GET THERE EVENTUALLY.

"KEEP DRIVING?" WHAT THE HELL KIND OF DIRECTION IS THAT?
I THOUGHT THESE SMALL TOWN FOLK WERE SUPPOSED TO BE ALL NORMAN ROCKWELL LIKE? I FEEL LIKE I'M IN AN EPISODE OF THE ***GODDAMN TWILIGHT ZONE*** FOR CRYING OUT LOUD!

Denio
McDermitt
140
MAYBE FRED WAS RIGHT.
MAYBE THIS IS A FOOL'S ERRAND I'M RUNNING.
I DON'T KNOW WHICH GETS ME IN MORE TROUBLE... MY AMBITION OR KNACK FOR BEING SO DAMNED THICK HEADED.
WHY DIDN'T I JUST KEEP MY MOUTH SHUT?
NO, LIKE AN IDIOT, I HAVE TO SAY THERE'S A STORY.
AND NOW WHAT?
I'M DRIVING AROUND AIMLESSLY IN THIS GOD-FORSAKEN DESERT WITH A QUARTER TANK OF GAS, PROBABLY CLOSER TO BREAKING DOWN THAN ACTUALLY FINDING A STORY.
80
Valmy
Gerlach
Smoke Creek
GOD, I'M AN IDIOT.
WHY DIDN'T I LET THE RENTAL AGENT TALK ME INTO THE DAMN GPS?
399
Lovelock
Pyramid Lake
Toulon
Message Status: Opened
Sent: Jun 16, 2006 9:20 PM
Deep truths are being kept. Government controls the information while the military suppresses it. They will stop at nothing to maintain secrecy. Sunset Diner... Carlson, Nevada... Wednesday at 5 PM. Full Disclosure!
SPACE
50
376
WHAT THE...?
Schurz
Gardnerville Ranchos
208
Smith Valley
208
95

JESUS! WHAT THE HELL HAPPENED HERE?
HELLO? ARE YOU... ARE YOU OKAY?
UN...
CHRIST! I'VE CALLED FOR HELP. I'M GONNA GET YOU OUT OF THERE.

IT'S HOT AS HELL IN HERE AND I SMELL FUEL. WE'VE GOTTA HURRY!
THE... COUGH... THE SEAT.
IT'S OKAY. I GOT THE SEATBELT. YOU'RE GONNA BE ALRIGHT.

DON'T WORRY ABOUT A THING. YOU'RE GOING TO BE OKAY.

HELP SHOULD BE HERE SHORTLY. JUST SIT TIGHT AND TRY NOT TO WORK YOURSELF UP.

IT'S THERE... EVERYTHING. IT'S ALL THERE.
WHAT IS? WHAT ARE YOU TALKING ABOUT?
THE SEAT... UNDER THE SEAT!
OKAY. OKAY. I'LL GET IT. JUST TRY AND STAY CALM.
WOOOO WOOOO

CHRIST!
WOOOO WOOOO
HU...COUGH... HURRY! THERE'S NOT MUCH... COUGH... NOT MUCH TIME!
WHAT THE HELL AM I DOING? I'M SUPPOSED TO BE OUT HERE FINDING A STORY, NOT BECOMING ONE!
WOOOO WOOOO

IS THIS WHAT YOU WANTED? AN ENVELOPE?
YOU HAVE TO... COUGH...

I HAVE TO WHAT?

LET THE WORLD KNOW.

SUNSET DINER
SERVING HOME COOKING SINCE 1937

ANOTHER COFFEE, SUGAH?
SURE... WHY NOT. THIRD CUPS THE CHARM, RIGHT?
YOU TRAVELING?
WHAT'S THAT?
I AIN'T SEEN YOU AROUND HERE BEFORE, SO I FIGURED YOU MUST JUST BE ON YOUR WAY THROUGH.
GENERALLY ANY NEW FACES WE SEE ARE JUST A PIT STOP.
YES AND NO. I'M DOWN FROM DENVER, BUT I WAS ACTUALLY SUPPOSED TO BE MEETING SOMEONE HERE.
CONSIDERING THEY'RE AN HOUR LATE, I'M GUESSING I'VE BEEN STOOD UP.
WELL, NOW THAT'S A DAMN NEAR CRIME IF YOU ASK ME. IN A SMALL TOWN LIKE THIS, A GOOD LOOKING MAN LIKE YOU HAS NO BUSINESS EATING DINNER BY HIMSELF.
WELL, I APPRECIATE THAT, BUT IT WASN'T A WOMAN WHO STOOD ME UP. I THINK IT WOULD HAVE BEEN LESS PAINFUL IF IT WAS.
NEEDLESS TO SAY, MY TRIP TO CARLSON HASN'T EXACTLY TURNED OUT AS PLANNED.
I'LL TELL YOU WHAT, LET ME PUT A LITTLE EXTRA TLC IN THAT NEXT CUP OF COFFEE OF YOURS AND WE'LL SEE IF WE CAN TAKE A LITTLE BIT OF THAT GLOOM OFF.
SOUNDS GOOD TO ME.
I'LL BE BACK IN TWO SHAKES THEN, SUGAH.

A DIARY?
THIS IS WHAT I RISKED MY LIFE FOR?
YOU TAKING NOTE OF YOUR BAD DAY, SUGAH?
NAH. I CAN BLOG WITH THE BEST OF THEM, BUT DIARIES AREN'T REALLY MY SPEED.
NO... SOMEONE GAVE THIS TO ME EARLIER TODAY. NOT SURE WHAT'S INSIDE, BUT MY GUESS IS IT WASN'T WORTH DRIVING A COUPLE HUNDRED MILES FOR.
WELL, YOU KNOW WHAT THEY SAY... SOMETIMES PEOPLE'S DIRTY LITTLE SECRETS ARE BETTER KEPT THAT WAY.
YOU THINK SO?
IF THEY WANTED THE WHOLE WORLD TO KNOW ABOUT WHAT WAS INSIDE, THEY WOULDN'T HAVE PUT IT IN THERE IN THE FIRST PLACE, NOW WOULD THEY?
I'LL KEEP THAT IN MIND.
SO LET'S SEE WHAT KIND OF DIRTY LITTLE SECRETS THE OLD MAN WAS HIDING.

OCTOBER 15, 1963
I RECENTLY ARRIVED HOME FROM A COMMANDING TOUR IN VIETNAM. MY HEAD FILLED WITH A CLOUD OF THOUGHTS... SOME GOOD, MOST BAD, I MADE MY WAY TO A PLACE THAT BROUGHT ME BACK TO MY YOUTH... THE SUNSET DINER.
Sunset DINER
SERVING HOME COOKING SINCE 1937
I GUESS IN MY OWN WAY, IT WAS AN ATTEMPT AT RECONNECTING WITH REALITY

IT'S THERE THAT I MET A CUTE WAITRESS WITH POUTY RED LIPS AND A SET OF LEGS THAT STARTED AND STOPPED IN PLACES I WANTED TO KNOW BETTER.
SO YOU'RE ONE OF UNCLE SAM'S BOYS, HUH?

I'D BEEN AWAY FOR A LONG TIME, AND AS FAR AS I'M CONCERNED... THERE'S NOTHING BETTER THAN AN AMERICAN GIRL WITH A STRONG SENSE OF WHO SHE IS AND WHAT SHE LIKES.
I'M ACTUALLY PILOT FOR THE AIR FORCE.

OOOH... A FLY BOY! YOU EVER SHOOT DOWN ANY COMMIES?
THAT'S CLASSIFIED, MISS, BUT I CAN TELL YOU THAT I'VE SECURED A LOT OF AIR SPACE IN MY DAY.
WELL THEN, I GUESS I SHOULD THANK YOU FOR KEEPIN ME SAFE, HUH?

JUST DOING MY DUTY. IF I MADE YOU SAFER IN THE PROCESS, THAT'S AN UNEXPECTED, YET EQUALLY GRATIFYING ADVANTAGE OF THE JOB.
AWAY FOR A LONG TIM OR NOT, TALKING TO A PRETTY YOUNG GIRL IS LIKE RIDING A BIKE... YO NEVER FORGET HOW T PEDDLE. AND BELIEVE ME, I CAN PEDDLE WIT THE BEST OF THEM.

WELL, IF YOU ASK ME, YOU DESERVE A FREE CUP OF COFFEE FOR ALL OF YOUR HARD WORK.

MUCH OBLIGED, MISS.
HAD IT NOT BEEN FOR A PAIR OF UNEXPECTED PARTY GUESTS, THAT LITTLE WAITRESS MAY HAVE ENDED UP MY WIFE SOMEDAY, BUT THOSE CARDS WEREN'T IN MY DECK.

FRIENDS OF YOURS?

CAN I ELP YOU, ELLAS?
YOU CAN HELP YOUR COUNTRY, SOLDIER.

YOUR PRESENCE IS REQUESTED IMMEDIATELY, COLONEL.
NOW IF YOU'LL JOIN US OUTSIDE, THERE'S A CAR WAITING.
WHEN SOMEONE FLASHES A BADGE OF THOSE CREDENTIALS, YOU GENERALLY LEAP WITHOUT WAITING FOR THEM TO TELL YOU HOW HIGH.
NEEDLESS TO SAY, ***I LEAPT***.

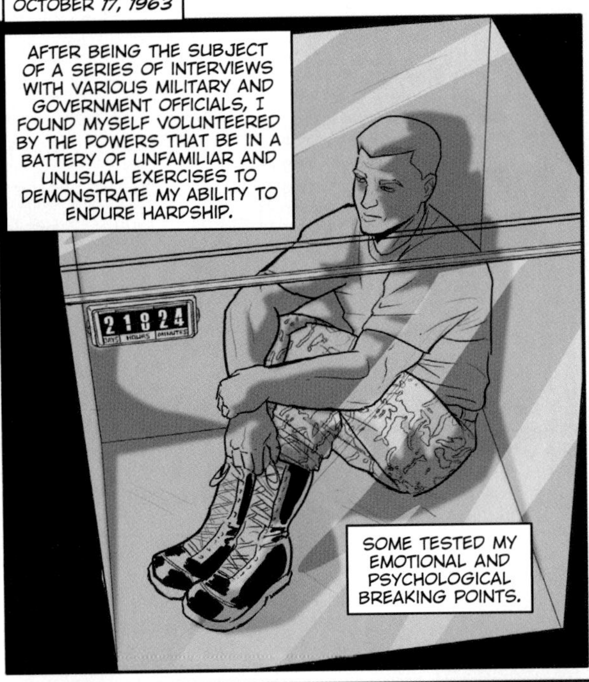
OCTOBER 17, 1963
AFTER BEING THE SUBJECT OF A SERIES OF INTERVIEWS WITH VARIOUS MILITARY AND GOVERNMENT OFFICIALS, I FOUND MYSELF VOLUNTEERED BY THE POWERS THAT BE IN A BATTERY OF UNFAMILIAR AND UNUSUAL EXERCISES TO DEMONSTRATE MY ABILITY TO ENDURE HARDSHIP.
SOME TESTED MY EMOTIONAL AND PSYCHOLOGICAL BREAKING POINTS.

WHILE OTHERS EVALUATED MY PHYSICAL ABILITIES IN EXTREME CONDITIONS, INCLUDING ZERO OXYGEN/ZERO GRAVITY ENVIRONMENTS.

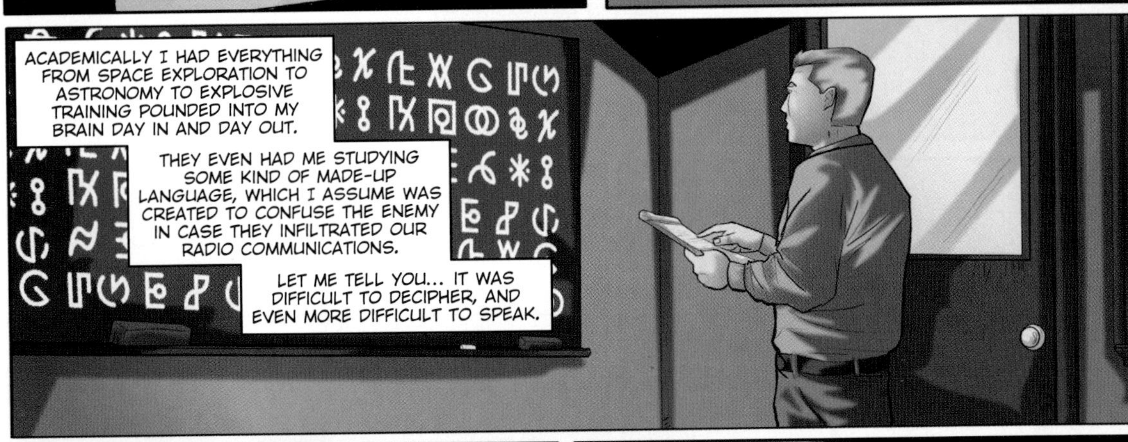
ACADEMICALLY I HAD EVERYTHING FROM SPACE EXPLORATION TO ASTRONOMY TO EXPLOSIVE TRAINING POUNDED INTO MY BRAIN DAY IN AND DAY OUT.
THEY EVEN HAD ME STUDYING SOME KIND OF MADE-UP LANGUAGE, WHICH I ASSUME WAS CREATED TO CONFUSE THE ENEMY IN CASE THEY INFILTRATED OUR RADIO COMMUNICATIONS.
LET ME TELL YOU... IT WAS DIFFICULT TO DECIPHER, AND EVEN MORE DIFFICULT TO SPEAK.

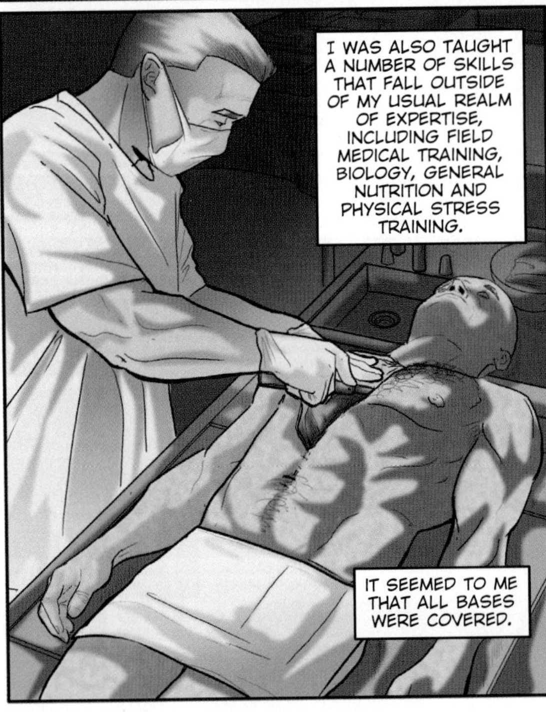
I WAS ALSO TAUGHT A NUMBER OF SKILLS THAT FALL OUTSIDE OF MY USUAL REALM OF EXPERTISE, INCLUDING FIELD MEDICAL TRAINING, BIOLOGY, GENERAL NUTRITION AND PHYSICAL STRESS TRAINING.
IT SEEMED TO ME THAT ALL BASES WERE COVERED.

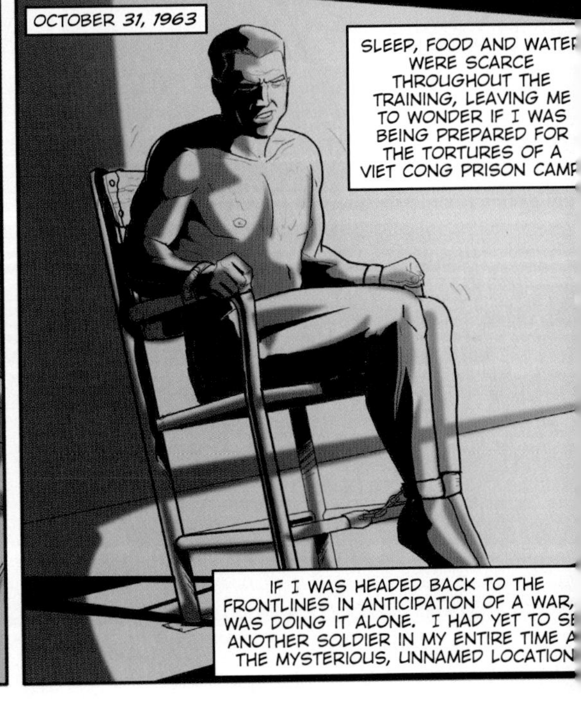
OCTOBER 31, 1963
SLEEP, FOOD AND WATE WERE SCARCE THROUGHOUT THE TRAINING, LEAVING ME TO WONDER IF I WAS BEING PREPARED FOR THE TORTURES OF A VIET CONG PRISON CAM
IF I WAS HEADED BACK TO THE FRONTLINES IN ANTICIPATION OF A WAR, WAS DOING IT ALONE. I HAD YET TO S ANOTHER SOLDIER IN MY ENTIRE TIME A THE MYSTERIOUS, UNNAMED LOCATION

NOVEMBER 1, 1963
MY PREVIOUS JOURNAL ENTRY HAS PROVEN TO BE PREMATURE. EARLIER TODAY I FOUND MYSELF STANDING IN A ROOM WITH ELEVEN OTHER INDIVIDUALS... NINE OF WHOM WERE MEN AND TWO WHO WERE WOMEN.
IT'S HERE THAT WE DISCOVERED THE NATURE OF THE TRAINING AND ULTIMATELY... THE OBJECTIVE. NEEDLESS TO SAY, NONE OF US WERE PREPARED OR EXPECTING WHAT FOLLOWED.

WELCOME TO CAMP PERRY, LADIES AND GENTLEMAN.
THE BUILDING YOU CURRENTLY STAND IN SERVES AS AN ABOVE TOP SECRET LOCATION. NOT EVEN THE HIGHEST LEVELS OF GOVERNMENT AND MILITARY HAVE KNOWLEDGE OF OR ACCESS TO IT.
YOU'VE BEEN CHOSEN TO SERVE YOUR COUNTRY UNLIKE ANY BEFORE YOU.
NOW PLEASE TAKE A FILE FROM THE TABLE AND WE CAN BEGIN BRIEFING YOU ON THE MISSION AT HAND.

IMMEDIATELY I WAS STRUCK BY THE CLASSIFICATION OF THE MISSION. ALTHOUGH IT COULD STAND FOR ANYTHING, SOMETHING TOLD ME THIS WAS NO LONGER A MATTER PERTAINING TO THE WAR.
PROJECT CRYSTAL KNIGHT
COSMIC TOP SECRET
WHAT YOU'RE HOLDING IN YOUR HANDS CONTAINS PERTINENT FACTS AND HISTORICAL INFORMATION RELATING TO PROJECT CRYSTAL KNIGHT.

YOU MAY HAVE HEARD OF AN INCIDENT THAT OCCURRED IN JULY OF 1947 ON THE OUTSKIRTS OF ROSWELL, NEW MEXICO. IT HAS BEEN REPORTED, AND SINCE REFUTED, THAT AN ALIEN SPACECRAFT CRASH LANDED IN NEARBY CORONA ON WHAT IS KNOWN AS THE FOSTER RANCH.
THE CRASH DID IN FACT OCCUR, AS DID ANOTHER AT NEARBY PELONA PEAK.
LAUNCH ESCAPE ASSEMBL
SERVICE MODULES

DURING A COMPLETE SWEEP OF THE CRASH SITES, SIX EXTRATERRESTRIAL BIOLOGICAL ENTITIES, HEREBY REFERRED TO AS EBE'S, WERE DISCOVERED AND TRANSPORTED TO LOS ALAMOS NATIONAL LABORATORY FOR FURTHER STUDY.
ONE WAS STILL *ALIVE.*
THE EBE REMAINED ALIVE UNTIL *1952.* DURING THAT TIME, COMMUNICATION WAS ESTABLISHED WITH THE BEING, AND MORE IMPORTANTLY, WITH ITS PLANET OF ORIGIN LOCATED IN THE ***ZETA RETICULI STAR SYSTEM.***
SINCE THAT TIME, WE HAVE BEEN IN CONTACT WITH THE SMALL PLANET.
DURING A SERIES OF CORRESPONDENCES, IT WAS AGREED THAT AN INTERPLANETARY EXCHANGE PROGRAM WOULD TAKE PLACE.
IT WAS DETERMINED THAT TWELVE MILITARY PERSONNEL WOULD TRAVEL TO THE ZETA RETICULI STAR SYSTEM AND LIVE AMONG ITS PEOPLE FOR TEN YEARS. YOU ARE THAT TEAM... TWO HIGH RANKING COMMANDERS, TWO EXPERIENCED PILOTS, TWO HIGHLY SKILLED LINGUISTIC SPECIALISTS, ONE MILITARY TRAINED BIOLOGIST, TWO DISTINGUISHED SCIENTISTS, TWO DOCTORS, AND A SECURITY OFFICER.
AS WE ALL TRIED TO ABSORB WHAT WE WERE BEING TOLD, A MEMBER OF THE GROUP SPOKE UP, ASKING WHAT WE ALL THOUGHT, BUT WERE TOO SHAKEN TO SPEAK OUT LOUD FOR OURSELVES.
WHAT IF WE DON'T WANT TO GO?
EACH OF YOU HAS CHOSEN TO SERVE THE UNITED STATES OF AMERICA, BUT THIS IS NOT AN ORDER BEING HANDED DOWN... ***IT'S AN HONOR.***
YOU ARE THE BEST OF THE BEST... THE TWELVE WE THINK MOST CAPABLE OF ACCOMPLISHING THE GREATEST EXPLORATION IN THE HISTORY OF MANKIND. YOUR EXPLOITS IN THE FARTHEST REACHES OF SPACE WILL BECOME ***LEGENDARY.***

MAKE NO MISTAKE, PROJECT CRYSTAL KNIGHT IS NOT WITHOUT ITS SHARE OF RISKS AND BECAUSE OF THIS WE ARE FORCED TO TAKE PRECAUTIONS IN THE EVENT YOU DO NOT RETURN.
IF YOU CHOOSE TO ACCEPT THE MISSION, EACH OF YOU WILL BE SHEEP-DIPPED. OFFICIALLY YOU WILL BE LISTED AS "MISSING," BUT TECHNICALLY YOU'LL NO LONGER EXIST.
NAMES, BIRTHDATES, BACKGROUNDS AND HOBBIES... IT MEANS NOTHING MOVING FORWARD.

EXCUSE ME, SUGAH, BUT IT'S TIME FOR US TO CLOSE UP FOR THE NIGHT.
IS YOUR DIARY FILLED WITH LOTS OF *JUICY* GOSSIP?

JUICY? NO. BUT IF WILDLY IMAGINATIVE IS WHAT YOU'RE LOOKING FOR, THIS IS IT.
WELL AT LEAST IT'S BEEN KEEPING YOU ENTERTAINED.

WELL, OLD MAN, LOOKS LIKE YOU'RE MY ENTERTAINMENT FOR THE NIGHT.

JULY 21, 1965
ALMOST TWO YEARS HAD PASSED BETWEEN THE INITIAL INTRODUCTION OF THE TEAM TO PROJECT CRYSTAL KNIGHT AND THE DAY OF THE ACTUAL EXCHANGE.
WITHIN THAT TIME FRAME WE WERE KEPT IN ISOLATION AT BOTH FT. LEAVENWORTH AND CAMP PERRY WHERE WE CONTINUED TO RECEIVE TRAINING PERTAINING TO THE MISSION, INCLUDING FURTHER ATTEMPTS AT UNDERSTANDING THE EBEN LANGUAGE, THOUGH ADMITTEDLY MOST OF US HAD A HARD TIME GRASPING IT.

TO MY SURPRISE I WAS PUT IN COMMAND OF THE TEAM.
WE WERE NO LONGER IDENTIFIED BY NAME AND INSTEAD GIVEN THREE-DIGIT NUMBERS.
I BECAME 102. OR AS 518 LIKED TO CALL ME... COMMANDER 102.
WE NEVER DEVIATED FROM USING THESE NUMBERS. IN MORE WAYS THAN ONE, THEY HELPED US MAINTAIN OUR IDENTITIES.

AS THE DOORS TO THE SPACECRAFT OPENED, IT BECAME CLEAR THAT ALL OF THE TRAINING COULDN'T PREPARE US FOR THE MOMENT OF TRUTH... THE MOMENT WE WERE TO SAY GOOD-BYE TO EARTH... HOME TO THE COUNTRY AND THE PEOPLE WE LOVED.
IT WAS THRILLING AND TERRIFYING ALL AT THE SAME TIME.

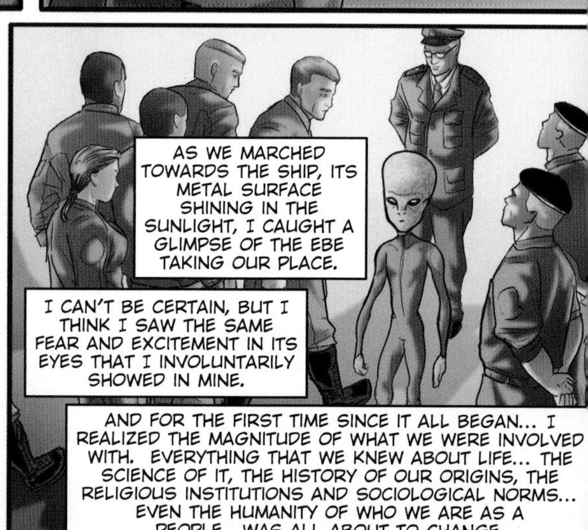
AS WE MARCHED TOWARDS THE SHIP, ITS METAL SURFACE SHINING IN THE SUNLIGHT, I CAUGHT A GLIMPSE OF THE EBE TAKING OUR PLACE.
I CAN'T BE CERTAIN, BUT I THINK I SAW THE SAME FEAR AND EXCITEMENT IN ITS EYES THAT I INVOLUNTARILY SHOWED IN MINE.
AND FOR THE FIRST TIME SINCE IT ALL BEGAN... I REALIZED THE MAGNITUDE OF WHAT WE WERE INVOLVED WITH. EVERYTHING THAT WE KNEW ABOUT LIFE... THE SCIENCE OF IT, THE HISTORY OF OUR ORIGINS, THE RELIGIOUS INSTITUTIONS AND SOCIOLOGICAL NORMS... EVEN THE HUMANITY OF WHO WE ARE AS A PEOPLE...WAS ALL ABOUT TO CHANGE.

MAN'S DISCOVERY OF FIRE LIT THE WAY FOR EVERYTHING WE KNOW OF THE PRESENT, BUT IT WILL BE THIS TEAM'S DISCOVERIES BEYOND THE STARS THAT WILL LIGHT THE WAY FOR THE FUTURE.

WE WERE VENTURING INTO UNEXPLORED TERRITORY, BOTH LITERALLY, AND IN EACH OF OUR OWN WAY, INTERNALLY AS WELL.

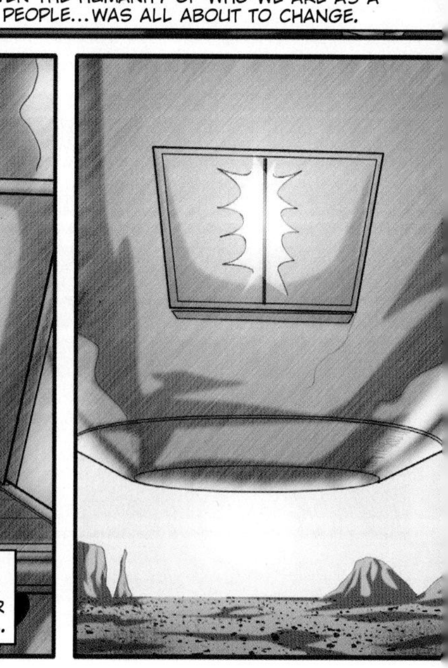

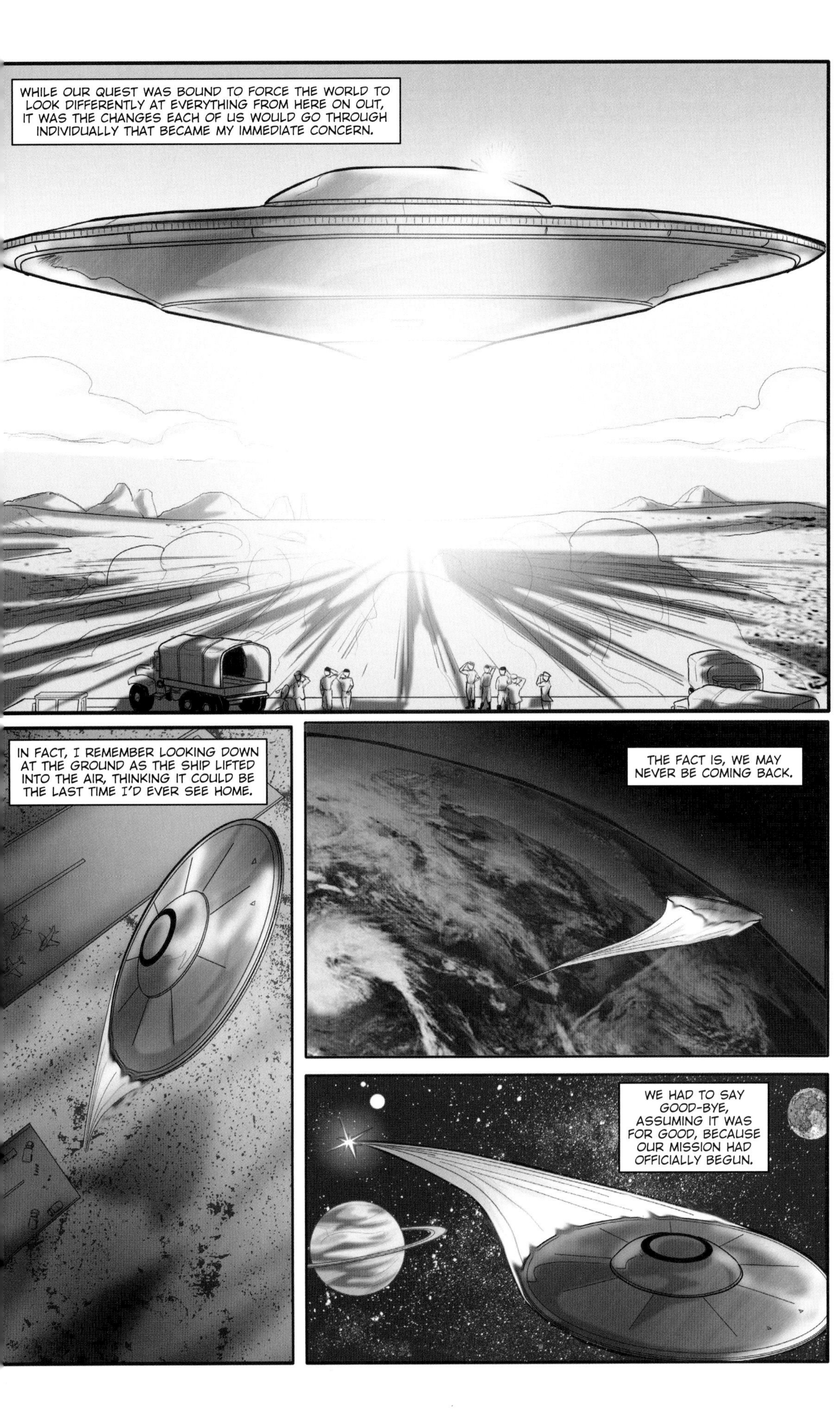
WHILE OUR QUEST WAS BOUND TO FORCE THE WORLD TO LOOK DIFFERENTLY AT EVERYTHING FROM HERE ON OUT, IT WAS THE CHANGES EACH OF US WOULD GO THROUGH INDIVIDUALLY THAT BECAME MY IMMEDIATE CONCERN.
IN FACT, I REMEMBER LOOKING DOWN AT THE GROUND AS THE SHIP LIFTED INTO THE AIR, THINKING IT COULD BE THE LAST TIME I'D EVER SEE HOME.
THE FACT IS, WE MAY NEVER BE COMING BACK.
WE HAD TO SAY GOOD-BYE, ASSUMING IT WAS FOR GOOD, BECAUSE OUR MISSION HAD OFFICIALLY BEGUN.

AFTER BOARDING THE SHIP, WE WERE ESCORTED TO A ROOM FILLED WITH A SERIES OF STRANGE PODS.
ALTHOUGH COMMUNICATION WITH THE EBES WAS DIFFICULT AND REQUIRED THE AID OF AN ALIEN COMMUNICATION DEVICE, WE SURMISED THAT THEY REQUIRED US TO ENTER THE PODS FOR OUR OWN SAFETY.
IN ORDER FOR OUR BODIES AND MINDS TO HANDLE THE LONG DISTANCE TRAVELED BETWEEN EARTH AND THE EBEN PLANET, WE WOULD NEED TO REMAIN IN A SORT OF SUSPENDED ANIMATION.
POD MUST GO.
AND WHILE THE EBES WERE UNUSUAL IN THEIR APPEARANCE AND MANNERISMS, THEY WERE SURPRISINGLY CORDIAL AND HELPFUL, THOUGH NOT EVERY TEAM MEMBER BELIEVED IN THEIR SINCERITY.
I SAY WE DON'T GET INTO THESE THINGS. WE DON'T HAVE ANY IDEA WHAT THEY DO.
I'D HAVE TO SAY THE OPPOSITE, SIR. I THINK WE'D BE IN GREATER DANGER IF WE DIDN'T GET INTO THEM.
SO IN YOUR EXPERT OPINION, *633*... ARE THERE ANY HEALTH OR SAFETY CONCERNS I SHOULD BE AWARE OF?
I'M NOT ENTIRELY SURE HOW THEY'RE POWERED, *102*, BUT THEY DO OMIT OXYGEN WITHIN THE CHAMBER... AND FROM WHAT I CAN TELL... THERE LOOKS TO BE A FILTERING SYSTEM THAT SERVES AS A WAY OF RECYCLING CARBON DIOXIDE.

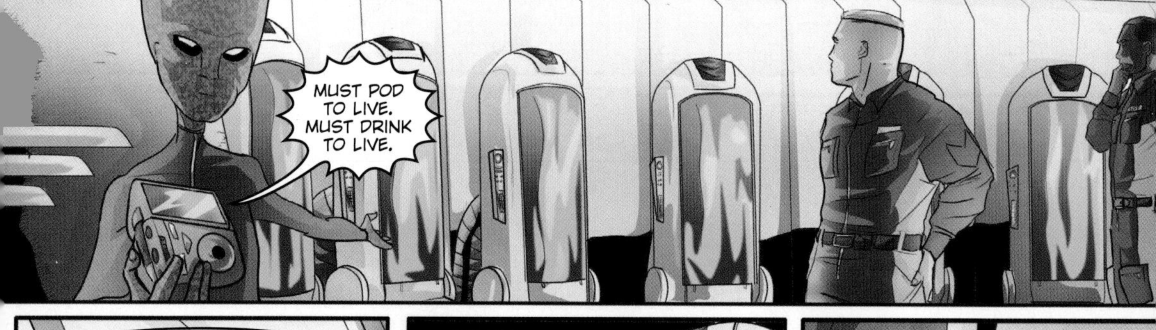
MUST POD TO LIVE. MUST DRINK TO LIVE.

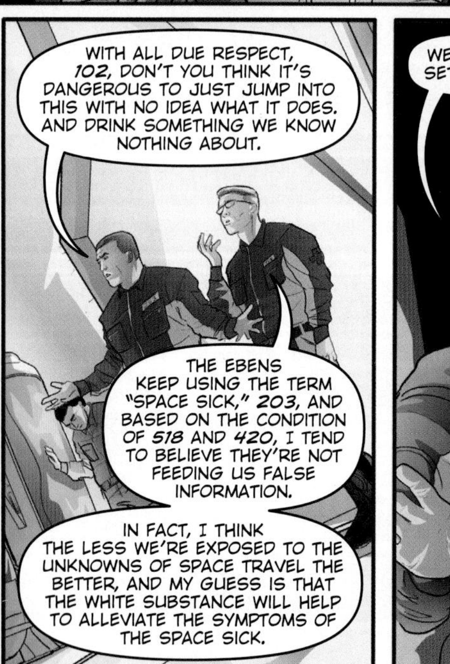
WITH ALL DUE RESPECT, *102*, DON'T YOU THINK IT'S DANGEROUS TO JUST JUMP INTO THIS WITH NO IDEA WHAT IT DOES. AND DRINK SOMETHING WE KNOW NOTHING ABOUT.
THE EBENS KEEP USING THE TERM "SPACE SICK," *203*, AND BASED ON THE CONDITION OF *518* AND *420*, I TEND TO BELIEVE THEY'RE NOT FEEDING US FALSE INFORMATION.
IN FACT, I THINK THE LESS WE'RE EXPOSED TO THE UNKNOWNS OF SPACE TRAVEL THE BETTER, AND MY GUESS IS THAT THE WHITE SUBSTANCE WILL HELP TO ALLEVIATE THE SYMPTOMS OF THE SPACE SICK.

WELL THAT SETTLES IT.
DRINK UP, PICK A POD AND MAKE FRIENDS WITH IT.
IT'S GOING TO BE YOUR HOME FOR THE NEXT HUNDRED MILLION MILES OR SO.

FOR WHAT IT'S WORTH, I'M WITH YOU ON THIS ONE, BUT THE CHAIN OF COMMAND PUTS MY ASS IN THE POD.

UNKNOWN DATE OF ENTRY.
WOKE TO ONE OF THE ES REMOVING THE TOP PORTION OF MY POD.
I HAVE NO SENSE OF TIME... ESPECIALLY HOW MUCH OF IT HAS PASSED SINCE MY LAST JOURNAL ENTRY, THOUGH I'M TOLD WE ARE NEARING THEIR HOME PLANET.

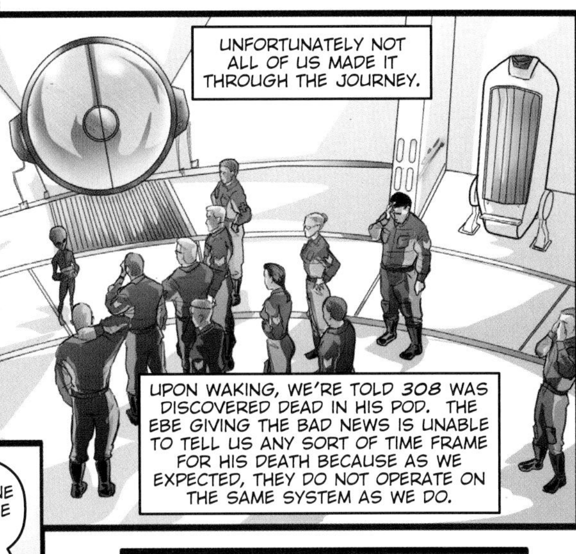

UNFORTUNATELY NOT ALL OF US MADE IT THROUGH THE JOURNEY.
UPON WAKING, WE'RE TOLD *308* WAS DISCOVERED DEAD IN HIS POD. THE EBE GIVING THE BAD NEWS IS UNABLE TO TELL US ANY SORT OF TIME FRAME FOR HIS DEATH BECAUSE AS WE EXPECTED, THEY DO NOT OPERATE ON THE SAME SYSTEM AS WE DO.

WEREN'T THEY MONITORING HIS ITALS? WHY DIDN'T THEY WAKE US?
WE'D LIKE TO SEE THE BODY.
IT'S OUR JOB TO EXAMINE IT AND FIND THE CAUSE OF DEATH.
WE COULD HAVE HELPED HIM! HE SHOULDN'T HAVE DIED. HELL, FOR ALL WE KNOW, HE MAY STILL BE ALIVE.

SILENCE YOURSELF, SOLDIER! DO I NEED TO REMIND YOU THAT *308* KNEW AND ACCEPTED THE RISKS OF THE MISSION?
WE ARE GUESTS. NOT HOSTAGES HERE. SETTLE DOWN BEFORE YOU MAKE MATTERS WORSE.

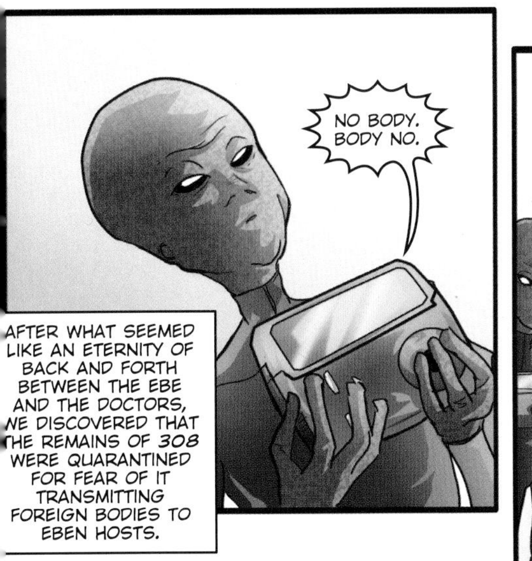

NO BODY. BODY NO.
AFTER WHAT SEEMED LIKE AN ETERNITY OF BACK AND FORTH BETWEEN THE EBE AND THE DOCTORS, WE DISCOVERED THAT THE REMAINS OF *308* WERE QUARANTINED FOR FEAR OF IT TRANSMITTING FOREIGN BODIES TO EBEN HOSTS.

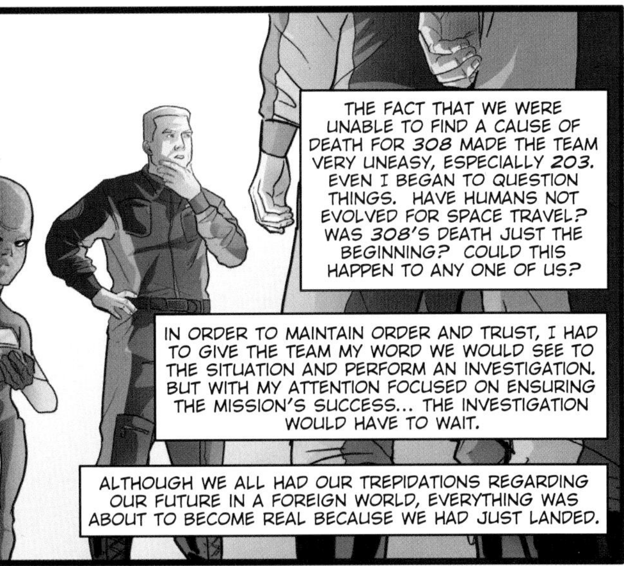

THE FACT THAT WE WERE UNABLE TO FIND A CAUSE OF DEATH FOR *308* MADE THE TEAM VERY UNEASY, ESPECIALLY ***203.*** EVEN I BEGAN TO QUESTION THINGS. HAVE HUMANS NOT EVOLVED FOR SPACE TRAVEL? WAS *308'S* DEATH JUST THE BEGINNING? COULD THIS HAPPEN TO ANY ONE OF US?
IN ORDER TO MAINTAIN ORDER AND TRUST, I HAD TO GIVE THE TEAM MY WORD WE WOULD SEE TO THE SITUATION AND PERFORM AN INVESTIGATION. BUT WITH MY ATTENTION FOCUSED ON ENSURING THE MISSION'S SUCCESS... THE INVESTIGATION WOULD HAVE TO WAIT.
ALTHOUGH WE ALL HAD OUR TREPIDATIONS REGARDING OUR FUTURE IN A FOREIGN WORLD, EVERYTHING WAS ABOUT TO BECOME REAL BECAUSE WE HAD JUST LANDED.

HOW DOES EVERYONE FEEL?
TO BE HONEST, I'M NOT FEELING ANY RESIDUAL EFFECTS OF THE SPACE SICK WHATSOEVER.
ME NEITHER. IN FACT, PHYSICALLY SPEAKING... I FEEL PRETTY GOOD.
HOW DO YOU IMAGINE IT... WHAT THE PLANET LOOKS LIKE?
MY GUESS IS LIKE NEW YORK CITY, BUT BIGGER AND MORE ADVANCED. WHAT ABOUT YOU?
WHEN I WAS IN THE POD, I DREAMT IT WOULD BE INCREDIBLY DIVERSE WITH AMAZING PLANT LIFE AND LANDSCAPES UNLIKE ANYTHING YOU CAN FIND BACK AT HOME.

I JUST HOPE ALL OUR TRAINING PAYS OFF. THERE'S NO TELLING WHAT THE ATMOSPHERE ITSELF COULD DO TO OUR PHYSIOLOGY. I'M KEEPING MY FINGERS CROSSED THAT WE'RE PREPARED FOR WHATEVER IS OUT THERE ONCE THESE DOORS OPEN.

LET'S JUST HOPE NONE OF US HAS TO TAKE THE *CYANIDE* WAY OUT.

I WANT EVERYONE ON THEIR GAME FROM HERE ON OUT. STAY ALERT AND WE STAY ALIVE.
AND NO MATTER WHAT, WE'VE GOT EACH OTHER'S BACKS.

WHEN THE DOORS OPENED, A COLLECTIVE SIGH FELL OVER THE TEAM.
I CAN'T SAY FOR CERTAIN WHAT THE OTHERS WERE THINKING, BUT MY INITIAL THOUGHTS WERE THAT THIS TECHNOLOGICALLY ADVANCED SOCIETY WAS MORE PRIMITIVE THAN I WOULD HAVE EVER EXPECTED.
I WAS SURPRISED AT HOW CRISP AND CLEAN THE AIR WAS.
THE SOUND OF SILENCE AMONGST THE EBEN PEOPLE PUZZLED MY EARS.
I WAS NO LONGER A SOLDIER, BUT A KID LOOKING AT THE WORLD FOR THE FIRST TIME.

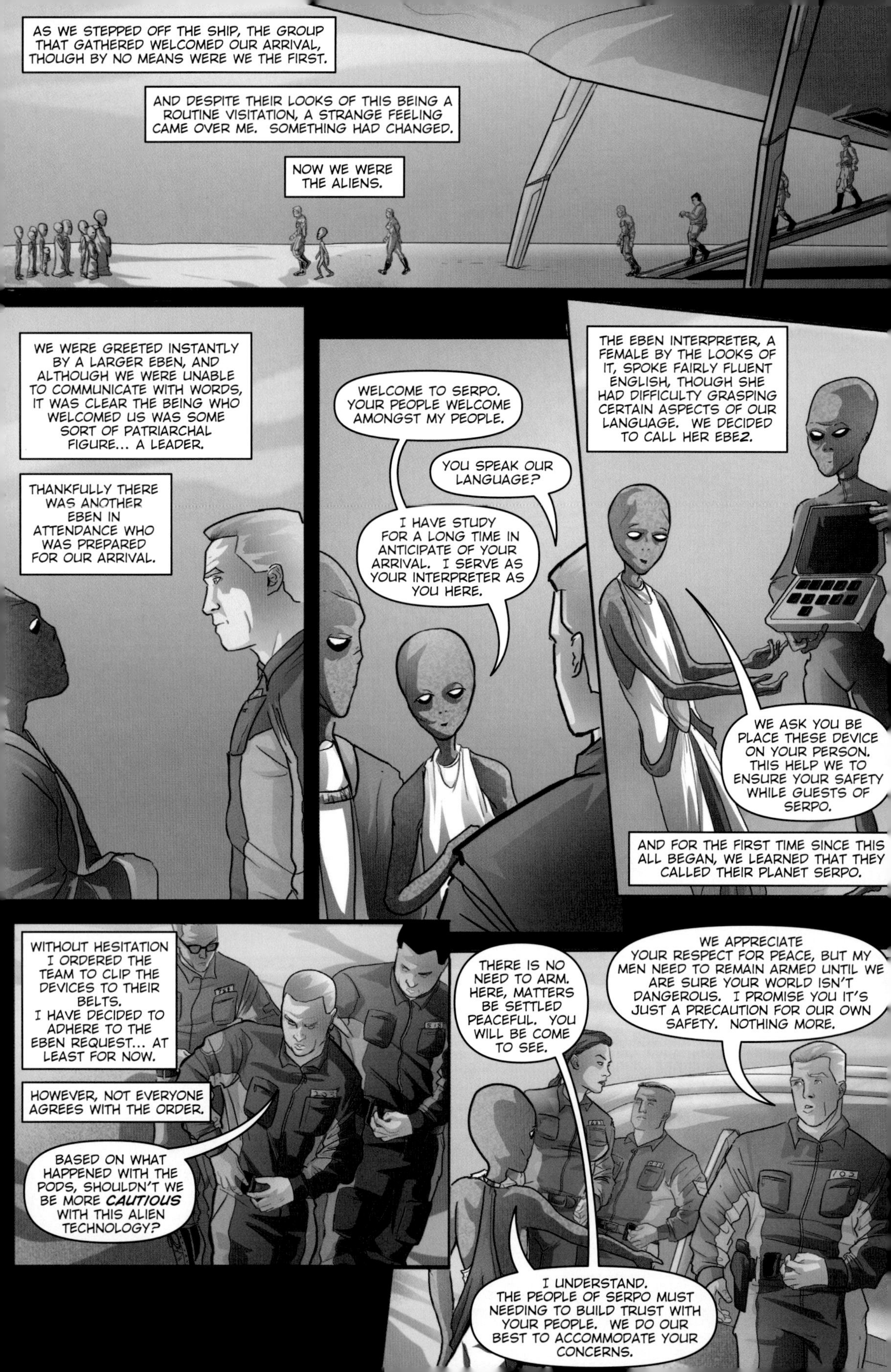
AS WE STEPPED OFF THE SHIP, THE GROUP THAT GATHERED WELCOMED OUR ARRIVAL, THOUGH BY NO MEANS WERE WE THE FIRST.
AND DESPITE THEIR LOOKS OF THIS BEING A ROUTINE VISITATION, A STRANGE FEELING CAME OVER ME. SOMETHING HAD CHANGED.
NOW WE WERE THE ALIENS.
WE WERE GREETED INSTANTLY BY A LARGER EBEN, AND ALTHOUGH WE WERE UNABLE TO COMMUNICATE WITH WORDS, IT WAS CLEAR THE BEING WHO WELCOMED US WAS SOME SORT OF PATRIARCHAL FIGURE... A LEADER.
THANKFULLY THERE WAS ANOTHER EBEN IN ATTENDANCE WHO WAS PREPARED FOR OUR ARRIVAL.
WELCOME TO SERPO. YOUR PEOPLE WELCOME AMONGST MY PEOPLE.
YOU SPEAK OUR LANGUAGE?
I HAVE STUDY FOR A LONG TIME IN ANTICIPATE OF YOUR ARRIVAL. I SERVE AS YOUR INTERPRETER AS YOU HERE.
THE EBEN INTERPRETER, A FEMALE BY THE LOOKS OF IT, SPOKE FAIRLY FLUENT ENGLISH, THOUGH SHE HAD DIFFICULTY GRASPING CERTAIN ASPECTS OF OUR LANGUAGE. WE DECIDED TO CALL HER EBE2.
WE ASK YOU BE PLACE THESE DEVICE ON YOUR PERSON. THIS HELP WE TO ENSURE YOUR SAFETY WHILE GUESTS OF SERPO.
AND FOR THE FIRST TIME SINCE THIS ALL BEGAN, WE LEARNED THAT THEY CALLED THEIR PLANET SERPO.
WITHOUT HESITATION I ORDERED THE TEAM TO CLIP THE DEVICES TO THEIR BELTS. I HAVE DECIDED TO ADHERE TO THE EBEN REQUEST... AT LEAST FOR NOW.
HOWEVER, NOT EVERYONE AGREES WITH THE ORDER.
BASED ON WHAT HAPPENED WITH THE PODS, SHOULDN'T WE BE MORE ***CAUTIOUS*** WITH THIS ALIEN TECHNOLOGY?
THERE IS NO NEED TO ARM. HERE, MATTERS BE SETTLED PEACEFUL. YOU WILL BE COME TO SEE.
WE APPRECIATE YOUR RESPECT FOR PEACE, BUT MY MEN NEED TO REMAIN ARMED UNTIL WE ARE SURE YOUR WORLD ISN'T DANGEROUS. I PROMISE YOU IT'S JUST A PRECAUTION FOR OUR OWN SAFETY. NOTHING MORE.
I UNDERSTAND. THE PEOPLE OF SERPO MUST NEEDING TO BUILD TRUST WITH YOUR PEOPLE. WE DO OUR BEST TO ACCOMMODATE YOUR CONCERNS.

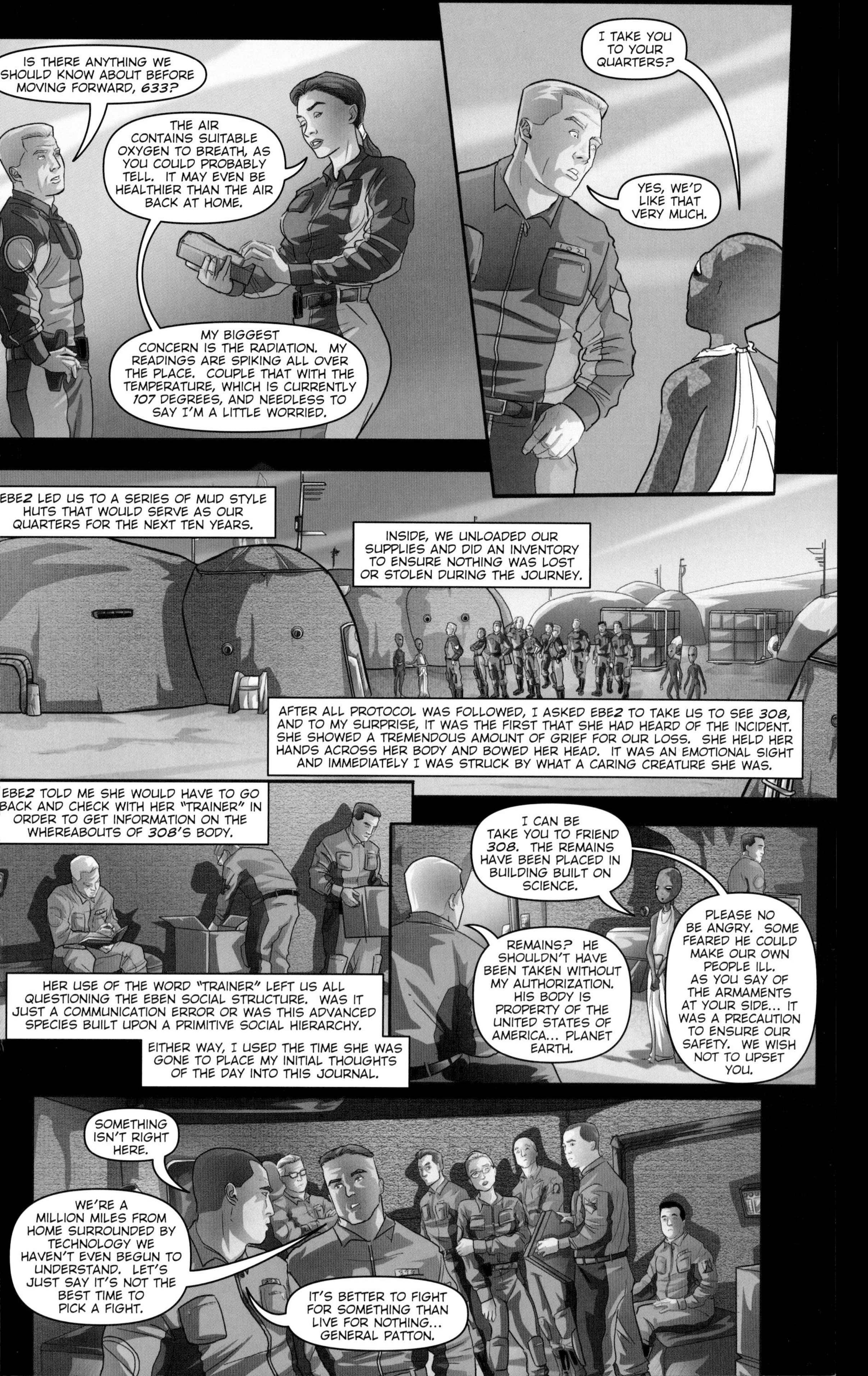
IS THERE ANYTHING WE SHOULD KNOW ABOUT BEFORE MOVING FORWARD, 633?
THE AIR CONTAINS SUITABLE OXYGEN TO BREATH, AS YOU COULD PROBABLY TELL. IT MAY EVEN BE HEALTHIER THAN THE AIR BACK AT HOME.
MY BIGGEST CONCERN IS THE RADIATION. MY READINGS ARE SPIKING ALL OVER THE PLACE. COUPLE THAT WITH THE TEMPERATURE, WHICH IS CURRENTLY 107 DEGREES, AND NEEDLESS TO SAY I'M A LITTLE WORRIED.
I TAKE YOU TO YOUR QUARTERS?
YES, WE'D LIKE THAT VERY MUCH.
EBE2 LED US TO A SERIES OF MUD STYLE HUTS THAT WOULD SERVE AS OUR QUARTERS FOR THE NEXT TEN YEARS.
INSIDE, WE UNLOADED OUR SUPPLIES AND DID AN INVENTORY TO ENSURE NOTHING WAS LOST OR STOLEN DURING THE JOURNEY.
AFTER ALL PROTOCOL WAS FOLLOWED, I ASKED EBE2 TO TAKE US TO SEE 308, AND TO MY SURPRISE, IT WAS THE FIRST THAT SHE HAD HEARD OF THE INCIDENT. SHE SHOWED A TREMENDOUS AMOUNT OF GRIEF FOR OUR LOSS. SHE HELD HER HANDS ACROSS HER BODY AND BOWED HER HEAD. IT WAS AN EMOTIONAL SIGHT AND IMMEDIATELY I WAS STRUCK BY WHAT A CARING CREATURE SHE WAS.
EBE2 TOLD ME SHE WOULD HAVE TO GO BACK AND CHECK WITH HER "TRAINER" IN ORDER TO GET INFORMATION ON THE WHEREABOUTS OF 308'S BODY.
HER USE OF THE WORD "TRAINER" LEFT US ALL QUESTIONING THE EBEN SOCIAL STRUCTURE. WAS IT JUST A COMMUNICATION ERROR OR WAS THIS ADVANCED SPECIES BUILT UPON A PRIMITIVE SOCIAL HIERARCHY.
EITHER WAY, I USED THE TIME SHE WAS GONE TO PLACE MY INITIAL THOUGHTS OF THE DAY INTO THIS JOURNAL.
I CAN BE TAKE YOU TO FRIEND 308. THE REMAINS HAVE BEEN PLACED IN BUILDING BUILT ON SCIENCE.
REMAINS? HE SHOULDN'T HAVE BEEN TAKEN WITHOUT MY AUTHORIZATION. HIS BODY IS PROPERTY OF THE UNITED STATES OF AMERICA... PLANET EARTH.
PLEASE NO BE ANGRY. SOME FEARED HE COULD MAKE OUR OWN PEOPLE ILL. AS YOU SAY OF THE ARMAMENTS AT YOUR SIDE... IT WAS A PRECAUTION TO ENSURE OUR SAFETY. WE WISH NOT TO UPSET YOU.
SOMETHING ISN'T RIGHT HERE.
WE'RE A MILLION MILES FROM HOME SURROUNDED BY TECHNOLOGY WE HAVEN'T EVEN BEGUN TO UNDERSTAND. LET'S JUST SAY IT'S NOT THE BEST TIME TO PICK A FIGHT.
IT'S BETTER TO FIGHT FOR SOMETHING THAN LIVE FOR NOTHING... GENERAL PATTON.

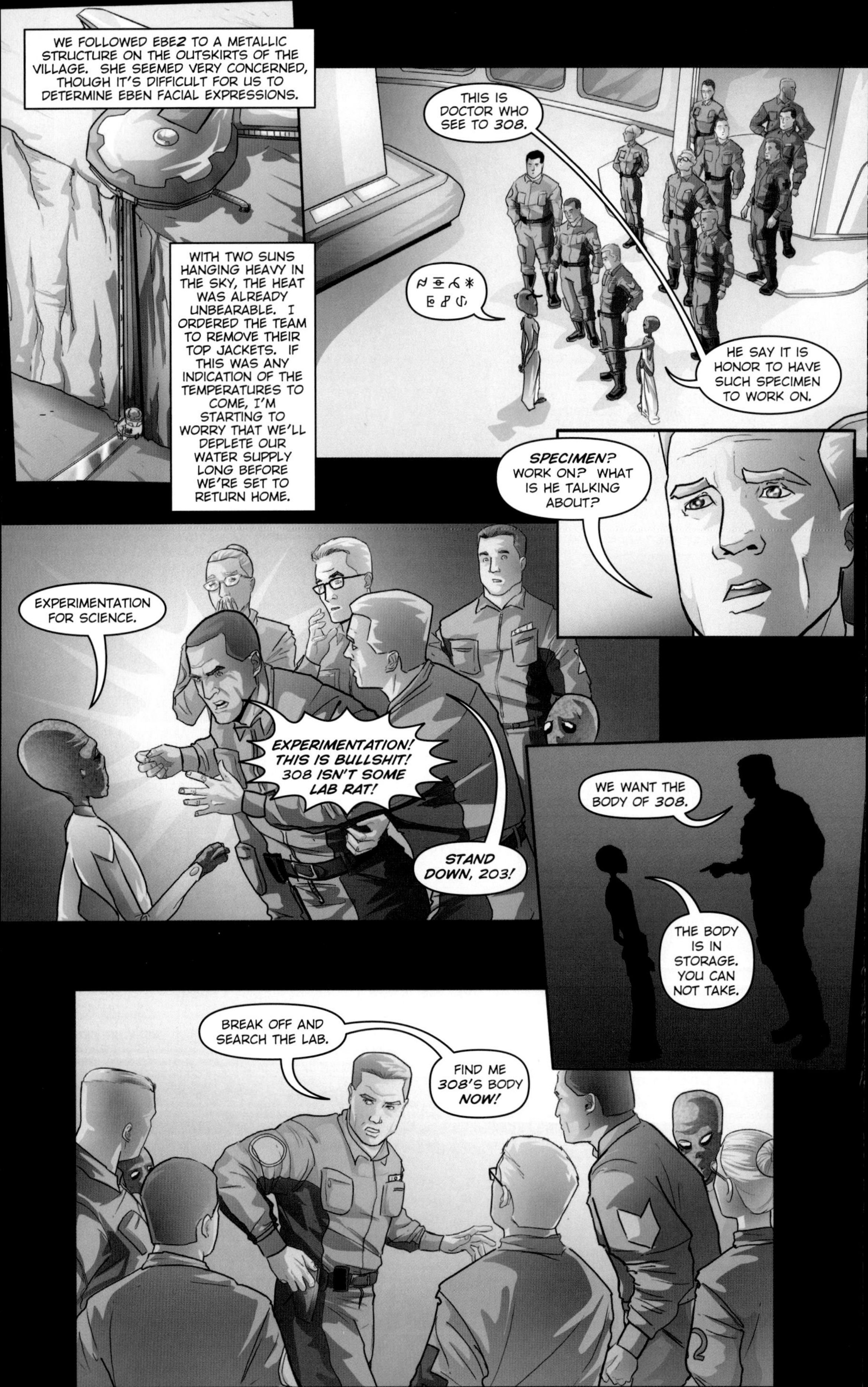
WE FOLLOWED EBE2 TO A METALLIC STRUCTURE ON THE OUTSKIRTS OF THE VILLAGE. SHE SEEMED VERY CONCERNED, THOUGH IT'S DIFFICULT FOR US TO DETERMINE EBEN FACIAL EXPRESSIONS.
WITH TWO SUNS HANGING HEAVY IN THE SKY, THE HEAT WAS ALREADY UNBEARABLE. I ORDERED THE TEAM TO REMOVE THEIR TOP JACKETS. IF THIS WAS ANY INDICATION OF THE TEMPERATURES TO COME, I'M STARTING TO WORRY THAT WE'LL DEPLETE OUR WATER SUPPLY LONG BEFORE WE'RE SET TO RETURN HOME.
THIS IS DOCTOR WHO SEE TO 308.
HE SAY IT IS HONOR TO HAVE SUCH SPECIMEN TO WORK ON.
SPECIMEN? WORK ON? WHAT IS HE TALKING ABOUT?
EXPERIMENTATION FOR SCIENCE.
EXPERIMENTATION! THIS IS BULLSHIT! 308 ISN'T SOME LAB RAT!
STAND DOWN, 203!
WE WANT THE BODY OF 308.
THE BODY IS IN STORAGE. YOU CAN NOT TAKE.
BREAK OFF AND SEARCH THE LAB.
FIND ME 308'S BODY NOW!

UPON ENTERING THE LABORATORY, I WAS IMMEDIATELY STRUCK BY WHAT SEEMED TO BE VARIOUS EBEN DOCTORS SCURRYING AROUND AISLE AFTER AISLE OF GLASS TUBS SEEING TO THE CONTENTS INSIDE.
MOST OF THEM WERE SURPRISED TO SEE US STANDING THERE. I KEEP FORGETTING THAT WE ARE THE ALIENS. I GUESS THIS IS A FEELING WE'LL EVENTUALLY GET USED TO.
I SENSED THE UNEASINESS OF MY TEAM AS WE SAW UNUSUAL EXPERIMENTS BEING PERFORMED. IN HOPES OF SETTLING NERVES, I ASKED EBE2 TO EXPLAIN THE PURPOSE OF THE LABORATORY.
THE ALIEN INTERPRETER TOLD US THAT THE BUILDING IS MEANT FOR GROWING CREATURES FROM OTHER PLANETS. WE DIDN'T UNDERSTAND THE TERM "GROWING," BUT SHE WENT ON TO TELL US THAT THE CREATURES IN THE TUBS WERE UNINTELLIGENT BEINGS... BEST DESCRIBED AS ANIMALS.
FROM HER EXPLANATION, WE WERE ABLE TO LEARN THAT THESE CREATURES WERE TAKEN FROM THEIR PLANETS FOR THE SOLE PURPOSE TO BE STUDIED. WITH MANY OF MY TEAM BEING RELIGIOUS AND ALL OF THEM MORALLY CENTERED, WE WERE STRUCK BY THE DARK SIDE OF THIS CIVILIZATION.
WE WERE ALL APPALLED THAT THIS ADVANCED SPECIES COULD BE CAPABLE OF EXPERIMENTS THAT SEEMED TO DEFY COMPASSION.
WHAT THE *HELL* IS THAT?
NO IDEA, BUT I WOULDN'T WANT TO SEE IT *AWAKE*, THAT'S FOR SURE.
WE DO NO UNDERSTAND YOU'RE UPSET. YOU ARE OUR GUESTS. WE WISH NOT TO OFFEND YOU.
I WANT THIS CONTAINER OPENED *NOW!*
HE SAYS NO TAKE BODY. CONTAINER LOCKED.

899 AND 661... RETURN TO THE HUTS AND GET SOME EXPLOSIVES.
THE REST OF US WILL STAY AND GUARD 308'S BODY.
I BEG NO GUNS. PLEASE... WE CAN MAKE BETTER. WE NOT WANT TO UPSET YOU!
YOUR PEOPLE HAD NO AUTHORITY TO EXPERIMENT ON ONE OF OURS.
I WILL NOT ALLOW YOUR PEOPLE TO COUNTERMAND MY DECISIONS. WE WILL TAKE HIM BACK OURSELVES.
WE ARE SORRY. WE DID NOT KNOW IT WOULD UPSET. PLEASE... NO GUNS. NO ANGER.
THE BODY WAS USED TO CREATE A HYBRID CLONE.
A CLONE?
THE SIGHT OF THE ALIEN-HUMAN CLONE BEING GROWN INSIDE THE CAPSULE TURNED MY STOMACH.
MY INSTINCT WAS TO SHOOT FIRST AND ASK QUESTIONS LATER, BUT 203 TOOK MATTERS INTO HIS OWN HANDS.

YOU'RE MONSTERS!
ABSOLUTE MONSTERS!

PLEASE, I BEG. EVERYONE SHOULD BE NICE.

I'M PUTTING AN END TO THIS NOW!
203! NO!
WITHOUT THINKING, 203 TRIED TO OPEN THE CAPSULE.
MEANWHILE, EBE2 PLEADED FOR HIM TO STOP, EXPLAINING THE CONTENTS OF THE CAPSULE WERE DANGEROUS... CHEMICALS THAT COULD HARM HIM.
THE MENTAL STRESS OF THE MISSION HAD FINALLY GOTTEN TO 203, HOWEVER, AND EITHER HE DIDN'T HEAR EBE2 OR HE DIDN'T CARE.
NEITHER I NOR THE REST OF THE TEAM COULD REACT IN TIME; THOUGH I'M NOT ENTIRELY SURE IT WAS INVOLUNTARY. EACH OF US WAS SHOCKED BY THE SIGHT OF 308'S DISSECTED BODY AND HIS ALIEN CLONE BEING GROWN IN A CAPSULE OF CHEMICALS.
THANKFULLY A NEARBY EBEN DOCTOR WAS ABLE TO INTERVENE BEFORE 203 COULD OPEN THE CAPSULE.
GET YOUR ALIEN HANDS OFF OF ME!
THOUGH LOOKING BACK, I'M SURE THE EBEN PHYSICIAN REGRETS THAT DECISION.
RESTRAIN 203!

THAT'S OUR OWN! HE'S ONE OF US! THIS IS INHUMANE!
GET HIM OUT OF HERE!
NOW!
I APOLOGIZE FOR 203'S OUTBURST. ARE YOU OKAY?
WE DO NOT WISH TO UPSET YOUR PEOPLE. WE DO NOT WISH SADNESS OVER OUR ACTIONS. I AM SO SORRY.
IT'S GOING TO BE ALRIGHT. I'M GOING TO MAKE SURE THIS GETS WORKED OUT.
I ASKED FOR PEACE. HIS ACTIONS NOT NECESSARY. NOT TOLERATE.
COUNCIL?
WHAT DO YOU MEAN?
STRIKING ANOTHER IS ACT OF AGGRESSION. THE COUNCIL WILL RESPOND.
WE ARE GOVERNED BY GROUP WHO ADMINISTER RULE.
I AM DEEPLY HURT BY THE FEELINGS WE CAUSE TO YOUR PEOPLE. VIOLENCE IS NEVER BE TOLERATED.
THE COUNCIL WILL ACT TO PUNISH AGGRESSION.
AND WITH THAT, I WRITE THIS ENTRY AS THE TEAM IS IMPRISONED WITHIN OUR OWN QUARTERS, GUARDED AND WATCHED BY MEMBERS OF THE EBEN MILITARY.
WE'VE BEEN ON SERPO FOR ONLY ONE DAY, AND ALREADY THE ENTIRE MISSION IS IN PERIL AND, VERY POSSIBLY, OUR LIVES.
EBE2 SAYS THE COUNCIL WILL MAKE A DECISION SHORTLY, SO FOR NOW WE WAIT.
OTHER THAN THAT, THERE'S NOTHING MORE WE CAN DO

CHAPTER TWO

WHAT THE HELL?
VRRRRRRRRRRRRROOM!
SHIT!
SHSSSSSSHH

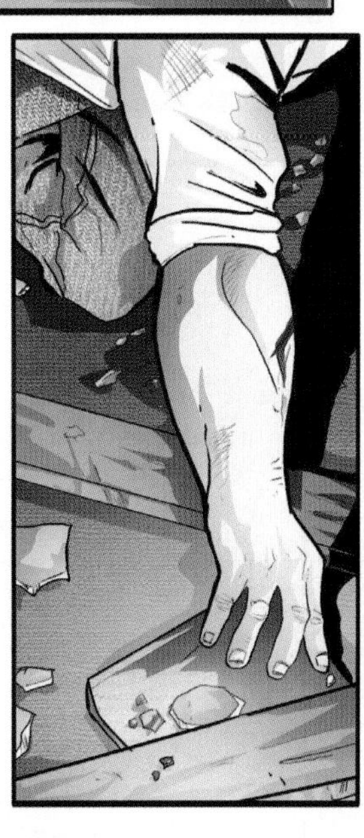

PFT
PFT

PFT
PFT
PFT
JESUS CHRIST!

SMASH!

SHIT!
MY KEYS!
SCREW IT!
WHAT THE HELL KIND OF DIRTY LITTLE SECRETS ARE YOU KEEPING IN HERE, YOU CRAZY OLD MAN?
HEY, FRED... IT'S CHARLIE. WHEN YOU GET THIS MESSAGE, GIVE ME A CALL ON MY CELL. I THINK I MIGHT HAVE STUMBLED ONTO A STORY OUT HERE THAT YOU'RE GOING TO WANT TO HEAR ABOUT.
IN FACT, IT MAY EVEN BE THE FRONT PAGE, ABOVE THE FOLD STORY YOU'VE BEEN LOOKING FOR.

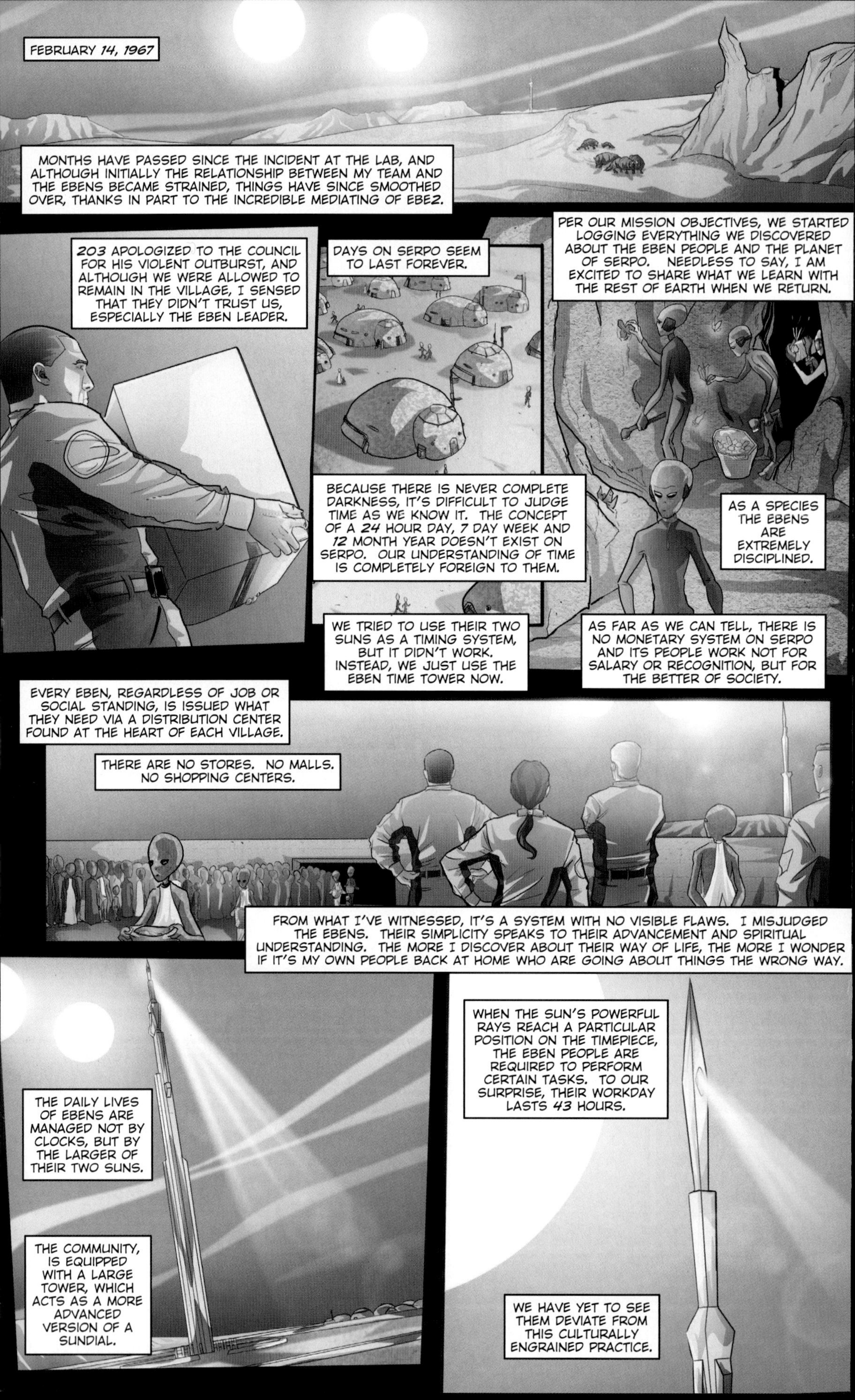
FEBRUARY 14, 1967
MONTHS HAVE PASSED SINCE THE INCIDENT AT THE LAB, AND ALTHOUGH INITIALLY THE RELATIONSHIP BETWEEN MY TEAM AND THE EBENS BECAME STRAINED, THINGS HAVE SINCE SMOOTHED OVER, THANKS IN PART TO THE INCREDIBLE MEDIATING OF EBE2.
203 APOLOGIZED TO THE COUNCIL FOR HIS VIOLENT OUTBURST, AND ALTHOUGH WE WERE ALLOWED TO REMAIN IN THE VILLAGE, I SENSED THAT THEY DIDN'T TRUST US, ESPECIALLY THE EBEN LEADER.
DAYS ON SERPO SEEM TO LAST FOREVER.
BECAUSE THERE IS NEVER COMPLETE DARKNESS, IT'S DIFFICULT TO JUDGE TIME AS WE KNOW IT. THE CONCEPT OF A 24 HOUR DAY, 7 DAY WEEK AND 12 MONTH YEAR DOESN'T EXIST ON SERPO. OUR UNDERSTANDING OF TIME IS COMPLETELY FOREIGN TO THEM.
WE TRIED TO USE THEIR TWO SUNS AS A TIMING SYSTEM, BUT IT DIDN'T WORK. INSTEAD, WE JUST USE THE EBEN TIME TOWER NOW.
PER OUR MISSION OBJECTIVES, WE STARTED LOGGING EVERYTHING WE DISCOVERED ABOUT THE EBEN PEOPLE AND THE PLANET OF SERPO. NEEDLESS TO SAY, I AM EXCITED TO SHARE WHAT WE LEARN WITH THE REST OF EARTH WHEN WE RETURN.
AS A SPECIES THE EBENS ARE EXTREMELY DISCIPLINED.
AS FAR AS WE CAN TELL, THERE IS NO MONETARY SYSTEM ON SERPO AND ITS PEOPLE WORK NOT FOR SALARY OR RECOGNITION, BUT FOR THE BETTER OF SOCIETY.
EVERY EBEN, REGARDLESS OF JOB OR SOCIAL STANDING, IS ISSUED WHAT THEY NEED VIA A DISTRIBUTION CENTER FOUND AT THE HEART OF EACH VILLAGE.
THERE ARE NO STORES. NO MALLS. NO SHOPPING CENTERS.
FROM WHAT I'VE WITNESSED, IT'S A SYSTEM WITH NO VISIBLE FLAWS. I MISJUDGED THE EBENS. THEIR SIMPLICITY SPEAKS TO THEIR ADVANCEMENT AND SPIRITUAL UNDERSTANDING. THE MORE I DISCOVER ABOUT THEIR WAY OF LIFE, THE MORE I WONDER IF IT'S MY OWN PEOPLE BACK AT HOME WHO ARE GOING ABOUT THINGS THE WRONG WAY.
THE DAILY LIVES OF EBENS ARE MANAGED NOT BY CLOCKS, BUT BY THE LARGER OF THEIR TWO SUNS.
THE COMMUNITY, IS EQUIPPED WITH A LARGE TOWER, WHICH ACTS AS A MORE ADVANCED VERSION OF A SUNDIAL.
WHEN THE SUN'S POWERFUL RAYS REACH A PARTICULAR POSITION ON THE TIMEPIECE, THE EBEN PEOPLE ARE REQUIRED TO PERFORM CERTAIN TASKS. TO OUR SURPRISE, THEIR WORKDAY LASTS 43 HOURS.
WE HAVE YET TO SEE THEM DEVIATE FROM THIS CULTURALLY ENGRAINED PRACTICE.

THE EBEN PEOPLE HAVE A VERY STABLE AND STRUCTURED SOCIETY.
EACH MALE HAD A FEMALE MATE, AND THEY ARE LIMITED TO ONE CHILD PER FAMILY UNIT.
THE EBENS HAVE ALLOWED US TO FULLY EXPERIENCE WHAT IT'S LIKE TO BE A PART OF THEIR CIVILIZATION, RIGHT DOWN TO LETTING US ATTEND A LIVE BIRTH.
WE HAVE WITNESSED FAMILIES WITH UP TO FOUR CHILDREN, BUT EBE2 WAS QUICK TO INFORM US THAT THOSE FAMILIES WERE CARING FOR EBEN OFFSPRING WHOSE PARENTAL UNITS WERE EITHER TRAVELING OR DECEASED.
SO FAR THE ONLY INTERFERENCE WE'VE RECEIVED IS WHEN WE'VE ATTEMPTED TO PHOTOGRAPH AN EBEN CHILD.
WE WERE CAUTIONED NOT TO DO IT AGAIN.
WE ENJOYED EBEN ENTERTAINMENT AT ITS BEST AND WORST AFTER BEING ASKED TO TAKE PART IN A GAME SIMILAR TO SOCCER.
BUT ULTIMATELY THE RULES WERE DIFFICULT TO FOLLOW AND THE GAME ITSELF PLAYED FOR AN ETERNITY.
WE HUMORED THE EBENS BY PLAYING ALONGSIDE OF THEM, BUT NONE OF US FULLY UNDERSTOOD THE GAME, NOR DID WE MUCH ENJOY IT.
YOUR SOCIETY IS SO TECHNOLOGICALLY POWERFUL, BUT AT THE SAME TIME SO PEACEFUL IN SPIRIT. WHY EVEN HAVE A MILITARY?
THERE WAS A GREAT WAR BETWEEN MY PEOPLE AND ANOTHER AND IT LAST FOR MANY FOREVERS. STILL THIS VERY DAY THEY SEEK US HARM AND LOOK TO DESTROY US.
THAT IS WHY WE KEEP EYES TO SKY ALL TIMES. TO BE SAFE WE MUST NEVER LET DOWN GUARD.
MARCH 27, 1967
WE ALL ENJOYED OURSELVES RECENTLY WHILE ATTENDING A RITUAL DANCE THAT EBE2 CALLED A REGULAR EVENT, CELEBRATED IN CONJUNCTION WITH A PARTICULAR WORK PERIOD.
THE EBENS DANCED TO AN ALMOST TRIBAL STYLE OF MUSIC, WHICH THEY PERFORMED USING THINGS SIMILAR TO DRUMS AND BELLS.
EVEN A FEW OF THE TEAM MEMBERS GOT IN ON THE ACTION, DOING THEIR BEST TO MIRROR THE ALIEN DANCE STEPS.

MARCH 29, 1967
FOR EVERY MEAL WE EAT ON SERPO, WE GATHERED IN WHAT EBE2 CALLS THE "EATING PLACE".
WHY DOES EVERYONE EAT IN A CHOW HALL?
CHOW HALL?
THIS BUILDING. WHY DO YOU ALL GATHER HERE INSTEAD OF EATING AT HOME?
WE ARE A SOCIAL PEOPLE. IT IS HOW WE KEEP CONNECTED AS ONE. WE CHOW TOGETHER ALWAYS.
I HAVE ENCOURAGED EACH TEAM MEMBER TO EAT AND DRINK THE EBEN OFFERINGS.
WHEN WE FIRST ARRIVED WE ATE ONLY ONE EBEN MEAL A DAY AT THE SUGGESTION OF 700. AT THE TIME, HE RECOMMENDED WE STICK TO OUR C-RATIONS SO OUR DIGESTIVE SYSTEMS COULD ADJUST TO THE UNFAMILIAR FOOD.
BUT HAVING BEEN HERE FOR AS LONG AS WE HAVE, WE ALL SEEM TO HAVE GROWN ACCUSTOMED TO THE ALIEN CHOW.
FOR THE MOST PART WE EAT SOMETHING SIMILAR TO COTTAGE CHEESE.
IT TASTES A LOT LIKE SOUR MILK, BUT AFTER YOU GIVE IT A FEW TRIES, IT'S NOT SO BAD.
OUR EXPERIENCE AT THE CHOW HALL WAS DIFFERENT TODAY, HOWEVER, BUT NOT BECAUSE OF THE FOOD.
TODAY WE WEREN'T THE ONLY ALIENS SAMPLING THE EBEN CUISINE.

IS THAT CREATURE... ONE OF YOUR KIND?
CREATURE? I NOT UNDERSTANDING THIS REFERENCE.
I'M SORRY. I DIDN'T MEAN TO OFFEND YOU. I JUST HAVE YET TO SEE ONE LIKE IT BEFORE.
NOT LIKE ME.
JUST VISITOR. LIKE YOU.
VISITOR FROM PLANET CORTA.
SHE LIKE YOU. TRAVEL FAR... MANY DISTANCES.
CORTA? WHERE IS THAT?

EBE2 WALKED ME TO THE CORNER OF THE CHOW HALL AND RAN HER HAND OVER A LARGE GLASS SCREEN. IT LOOKS LIKE A TELEVISION, BUT VERY THIN... TOO THIN TO CONTAIN CATHODE TUBES, TRANSISTORS OR ELECTRONICS. I DON'T KNOW HOW IT OPERATES, BUT INSTANTLY A VAST MAP OF THE UNIVERSE APPEARED.
CORTA. HOME OF HER.
AND EARTH?

EARTH.
MANY VISITORS COME TO SERPO. SOME FRIENDLY. SOME NOT.

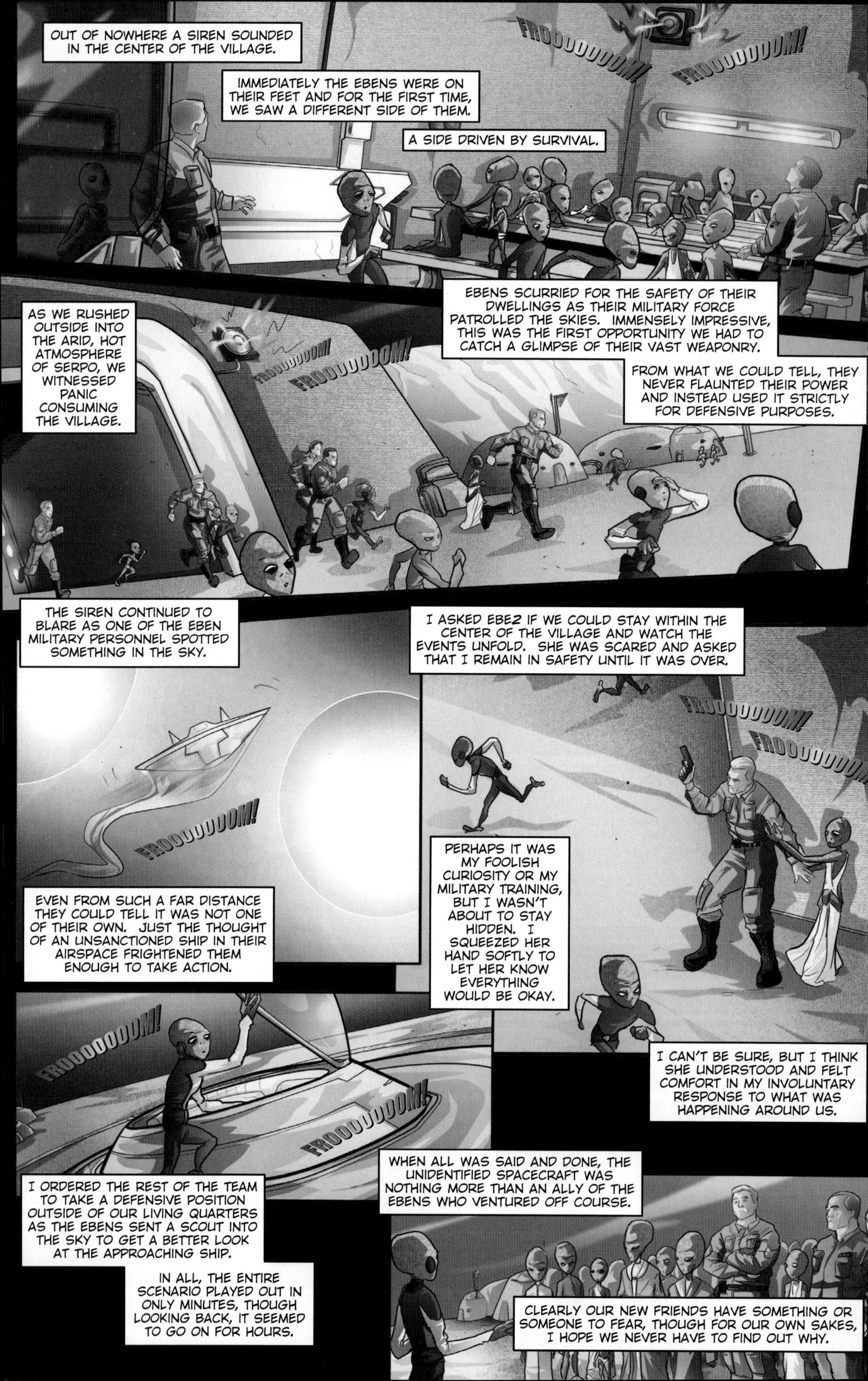
OUT OF NOWHERE A SIREN SOUNDED IN THE CENTER OF THE VILLAGE.
FROOOOOOOOM!
FROOOOOOOOM!
IMMEDIATELY THE EBENS WERE ON THEIR FEET AND FOR THE FIRST TIME, WE SAW A DIFFERENT SIDE OF THEM.
A SIDE DRIVEN BY SURVIVAL.
AS WE RUSHED OUTSIDE INTO THE ARID, HOT ATMOSPHERE OF SERPO, WE WITNESSED PANIC CONSUMING THE VILLAGE.
FROOOOOOOOM!
FROOOOOOOOM!
EBENS SCURRIED FOR THE SAFETY OF THEIR DWELLINGS AS THEIR MILITARY FORCE PATROLLED THE SKIES. IMMENSELY IMPRESSIVE, THIS WAS THE FIRST OPPORTUNITY WE HAD TO CATCH A GLIMPSE OF THEIR VAST WEAPONRY.
FROM WHAT WE COULD TELL, THEY NEVER FLAUNTED THEIR POWER AND INSTEAD USED IT STRICTLY FOR DEFENSIVE PURPOSES.
THE SIREN CONTINUED TO BLARE AS ONE OF THE EBEN MILITARY PERSONNEL SPOTTED SOMETHING IN THE SKY.
FROOOOOOOOM!
EVEN FROM SUCH A FAR DISTANCE THEY COULD TELL IT WAS NOT ONE OF THEIR OWN. JUST THE THOUGHT OF AN UNSANCTIONED SHIP IN THEIR AIRSPACE FRIGHTENED THEM ENOUGH TO TAKE ACTION.
I ASKED EBE2 IF WE COULD STAY WITHIN THE CENTER OF THE VILLAGE AND WATCH THE EVENTS UNFOLD. SHE WAS SCARED AND ASKED THAT I REMAIN IN SAFETY UNTIL IT WAS OVER.
FROOOOOOOOM!
PERHAPS IT WAS MY FOOLISH CURIOSITY OR MY MILITARY TRAINING, BUT I WASN'T ABOUT TO STAY HIDDEN. I SQUEEZED HER HAND SOFTLY TO LET HER KNOW EVERYTHING WOULD BE OKAY.
I CAN'T BE SURE, BUT I THINK SHE UNDERSTOOD AND FELT COMFORT IN MY INVOLUNTARY RESPONSE TO WHAT WAS HAPPENING AROUND US.
FROOOOOOOOM!
FROOOOOOOOM!
I ORDERED THE REST OF THE TEAM TO TAKE A DEFENSIVE POSITION OUTSIDE OF OUR LIVING QUARTERS AS THE EBENS SENT A SCOUT INTO THE SKY TO GET A BETTER LOOK AT THE APPROACHING SHIP.
IN ALL, THE ENTIRE SCENARIO PLAYED OUT IN ONLY MINUTES, THOUGH LOOKING BACK, IT SEEMED TO GO ON FOR HOURS.
WHEN ALL WAS SAID AND DONE, THE UNIDENTIFIED SPACECRAFT WAS NOTHING MORE THAN AN ALLY OF THE EBENS WHO VENTURED OFF COURSE.
CLEARLY OUR NEW FRIENDS HAVE SOMETHING OR SOMEONE TO FEAR, THOUGH FOR OUR OWN SAKES, I HOPE WE NEVER HAVE TO FIND OUT WHY.

JULY 9TH, 1967
HAVING SPENT SO MUCH TIME WITH EBE2, I'VE DEVELOPED AN ENORMOUS SENSE OF RESPECT AND REVERENCE FOR HER. MORE THAN I HAVE WITH ANY HUMAN.
ALTHOUGH WE ARE WORLDS APART, I ENJOY BEING IN HER COMPANY. HER WISDOM AND OUTLOOK OF THE UNIVERSE SOMEHOW SEEM TO MAKE ME A BETTER PERSON.
WHAT DO YOU DO?
ME? OH... JUST BEING A GOOD SOLDIER, I SUPPOSE. I GUESS SOMETIMES IT'S HARD TO BREAK HABITS, EVEN ON SERPO.
I SEE.
YOU KNOW, YOU DON'T ALWAYS HAVE TO KEEP AN EYE ON US. IF YOU HAVE OTHER THINGS TO DO, I'M SURE WE'LL BE FINE TO TAKE CARE OF OURSELVES FOR AWHILE.
YOU DO NOT WISH MY COMPANY?
THAT'S NOT IT ALL. I JUST FEEL BAD THAT WE'RE TAKING UP ALL OF YOUR TIME.
PLEASE DON'T FEEL BAD. I MAKE CHOICE TO BE HERE. I ENJOY 102'S COMPANY.
WELL IN THAT CASE, WHY DON'T YOU PULL UP A PILE OF SERPO?
A PILE OF SERPO?
OH... SORRY. IT'S JUST A SAYING WE HAVE BACK ON EARTH. BASICALLY, I'M INVITING YOU TO HAVE A SEAT.
OUR DOCTORS NEED TO TAKE HUMAN HEALTH FLUID FOR STUDY OF MEDICINE SHOULD ANY OF YOU NEED IT.
YOU MEAN BLOOD?
YES. YOUR HEALTH FLUID IS DIFFERENT. MEDICINES MUST BE DIFFERENT TOO.
I'LL SPEAK WITH MY TEAM, BUT I'M SURE THEY'LL HAVE CONCERNS.
I ASSURE YOU BLOOD NOT WANTED TO MAKE ANOTHER. JUST TO MAKE YOU BETTER IF BECOME SICK.
IT'S OKAY. I TRUST YOU.

JULY 10TH, 1967
THE EBEN DOCTORS HAVE REQUESTED WE SUPPLY THEM WITH BLOOD SAMPLES FROM EACH OF US.
THEY WILL USE IT TO MAKE MEDICINE SHOULD ANY OF US BECOME SICK OR INJURED.
AND YOU *BELIEVE THAT?*
I DON'T HAVE ANY REASON NOT TO, *203.* THEY'VE BEEN NOTHING BUT OPEN WITH US SINCE WE GOT HERE.
I HAVE TO AGREE WITH *203.* HOW DO WE KNOW THEY WON'T USE IT TO CLONE MORE OF THOSE HYBRID CREATURES WE SAW IN THE LAB?

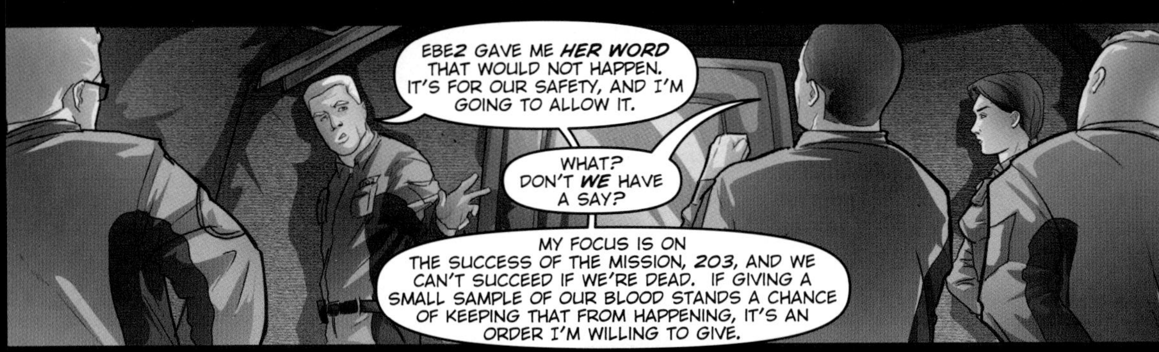
EBE2 GAVE ME ***HER WORD*** THAT WOULD NOT HAPPEN. IT'S FOR OUR SAFETY, AND I'M GOING TO ALLOW IT.
WHAT? DON'T ***WE*** HAVE A SAY?
MY FOCUS IS ON THE SUCCESS OF THE MISSION, *203,* AND WE CAN'T SUCCEED IF WE'RE DEAD. IF GIVING A SMALL SAMPLE OF OUR BLOOD STANDS A CHANCE OF KEEPING THAT FROM HAPPENING, IT'S AN ORDER I'M WILLING TO GIVE.

NEEDLESS TO SAY, NOT EVERYONE AGREED WITH MY DECISION TO ALLOW THE EBENS TO DRAW BLOOD SAMPLES, BUT THIS ISN'T A DEMOCRACY.

I'M DOING WHAT I HAVE TO.

CAN I ASK YOU SOMETHING?
CERTAINLY. I BE HERE TO ANSWER YOUR QUESTIONS ALWAYS.
I WAS JUST CURIOUS ABOUT THE ONE THAT TOOK OUR PLACE... THE ONE WHO WENT TO MY PLANET?
HIS NAME, LIKE MINE, NOT SOMETHING FOR YOUR PEOPLE TO SAY. A SOUND, NOT A WORD.
WHAT IS HE LIKE?
HE IS MILITARY LIKE YOU, ***YET DIFFERENT.***
QUIET. RESERVED. YOU BOTH HAVE INTEREST IN FINDING NEWNESS IN UNIVERSE.
HE GOOD INSIDE LIKE YOU.
WELL THEN I'M ***HONORED*** TO HAVE THE COMPARISON MADE.
I WISH HIM WELLNESS IN HIS JOURNEY.
YOU DON'T HAVE TO WORRY ABOUT THAT. I HAVE NO DOUBT MY GOVERNMENT IS TREATING HIM WITH THE ***UTMOST RESPECT AND KINDNESS.***

JULY 10TH, 1967
LOS ALAMOS
AIR FORCE
BASE
WARNING
RESTRICTED AREA
NO TRESPASSING
BEYOND THIS POINT

DO NOT
ENTER
USE OF
DEADLY
FORCE
AUTHORIZED

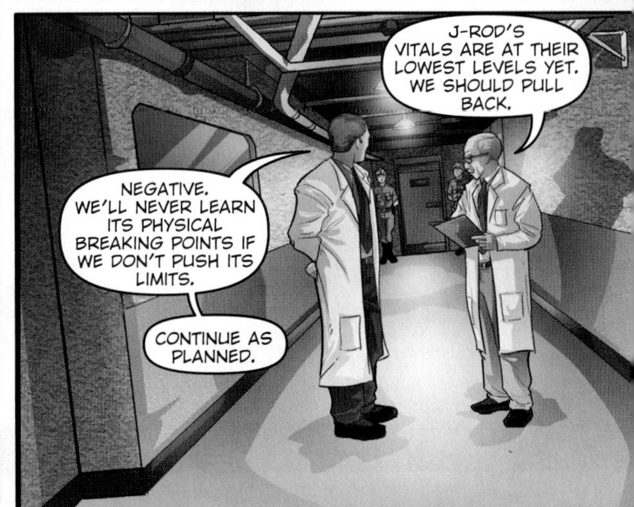
J-ROD'S VITALS ARE AT THEIR LOWEST LEVELS YET. WE SHOULD PULL BACK.
NEGATIVE. WE'LL NEVER LEARN ITS PHYSICAL BREAKING POINTS IF WE DON'T PUSH ITS LIMITS.
CONTINUE AS PLANNED.

DECEMBER 1, 1967
ALTHOUGH IT'S ALWAYS LIGHT OUTSIDE, THE TEAM HAS MANAGED TO WORK UP A SCHEDULE WHERE WE SLEEP AT SPECIFIC TIMES SO NOT TO CONFUSE OUR BODIES AND LEAVE OURSELVES SUSCEPTIBLE TO A WEAKENED IMMUNE SYSTEM.
IT WAS DIFFICULT FOR EVERYONE AT FIRST, BUT IN TIME WE ALL GOT USED TO SLEEPING WITH THE SUNLIGHT BEATING DOWN ON OUR HUT.
BUT REGARDLESS OF HOW HARDENED OUR MINDS AND BODIES BECOME, SOME THINGS ARE JUST IMPOSSIBLE TO SLEEP THROUGH.
KAROOOOOOOOOM!!

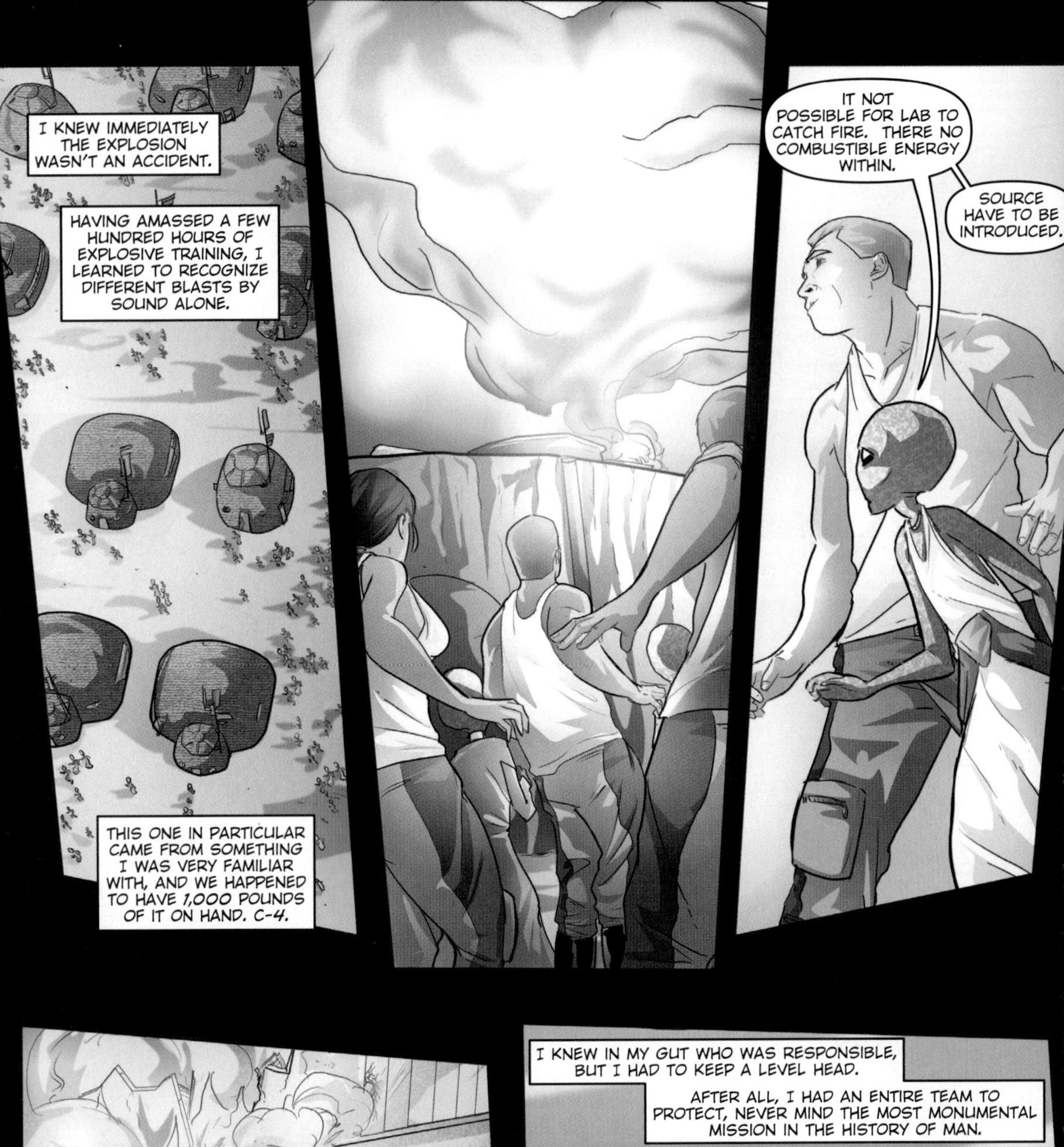
I KNEW IMMEDIATELY THE EXPLOSION WASN'T AN ACCIDENT.
HAVING AMASSED A FEW HUNDRED HOURS OF EXPLOSIVE TRAINING, I LEARNED TO RECOGNIZE DIFFERENT BLASTS BY SOUND ALONE.
THIS ONE IN PARTICULAR CAME FROM SOMETHING I WAS VERY FAMILIAR WITH, AND WE HAPPENED TO HAVE 1,000 POUNDS OF IT ON HAND. C-4.
IT NOT POSSIBLE FOR LAB TO CATCH FIRE. THERE NO COMBUSTIBLE ENERGY WITHIN.
SOURCE HAVE TO BE INTRODUCED.

I KNEW IN MY GUT WHO WAS RESPONSIBLE, BUT I HAD TO KEEP A LEVEL HEAD.
AFTER ALL, I HAD AN ENTIRE TEAM TO PROTECT, NEVER MIND THE MOST MONUMENTAL MISSION IN THE HISTORY OF MAN.
UNFORTUNATELY, I WASN'T THE ONLY ONE THINKING WITH MY GUT.

HE SEA OF EBENS PARTED AS THEIR COUNCIL LEADER MARCHED TOWARDS US.
CONSIDERING THIS WAS THE FIRST TIME WE HAD SEEN HIM WITH A MILITARY ESCORT, I KNEW THINGS WERE ABOUT TO TAKE A DRAMATIC TURN FOR THE WORSE.
WHAT DID HE SAY?
HE SAYS HUMANS MAKE LAB CATCHING FIRE.
YOU HAVE NO PROOF OF THAT!
HE ASKS TO KNOW WHY?

I TOLD HIM HIS ACCUSATION UNTRUE.
I TOLD HIM YOU ARE GOOD INSIDE... INCAPABLE OF SUCH ACT OF AGGRESSION.

HE SAYS VISITORS FROM EARTH CAN ***NO LONGER TRUST.***
YOU MAY STAY IN VILLAGE ***NO MORE.***

REGARDLESS OF OUR ATTEMPTS TO CHANGE THE COUNCIL'S DECISION, IT WAS CLEAR WE WERE NO LONGER WELCOME AMONGST THE EBENS.

OUR MISSION HAD BEEN COMPROMISED.

WHY'D YOU DO IT!?!?

AT LEAST GIVE ME THE COMMON COURTESY OF A RESPONSE, YOU SON OF A BITCH.
WHAT HAPPENED DOESN'T NEED A RESPONSE.

SOMEONE HAD TO DO SOMETHING. I WASN'T GOING TO LET THEM USE OUR BLOOD IN THAT LAB TO MAKE SOME KIND OF A HYBRID FREAK LIKE THEY DID WITH 308.
THAT'S NOT WHAT THEY'RE DOING AND YOU KNOW IT!
THAT'S BULLSHIT. YOU HAVE NO IDEA WHAT THEY'RE DOING IN THERE. YOU ACT MORE LIKE ONE OF THEM THAN A COMMANDER OF THE UNITED STATES AIR FORCE!
YOU BETTER WATCH YOUR TONGUE, SOLDIER!
WHAT THEY'RE DOING... IT ISN'T RIGHT. WHY AM I THE ONLY ONE WHO SEES THAT?
BECAUSE YOU'RE SO HELL BENT ON BEING A COWBOY THAT YOU'RE BLIND TO WHAT'S GOING ON AROUND YOU! THE EBENS ARE A SOPHISTICATED AND COMPASSIONATE SPECIES.
YOU NEED TO ASK YOURSELF WHY YOU'RE THE ONLY ONE WHO CAN SEE THAT!
KAFROOOOOOOM!

THE ATTACK CAME WITHOUT WARNING. THIS TIME THERE WAS NO SIREN.
I SAW SPACESHIPS FIRING LASER BEAMS AND ALIENS USING STRANGE WEAPONS TO DEFEND THEMSELVES AND THEIR LOVED ONES.
THE WHOLE THING WAS LIKE SOME SURREAL IMAGE THAT ONLY I COULD SEE.
BUT AS I WATCHED MY IMAGINATION PLAY OUT IN FRONT OF MY EYES, I REALIZED THE EBENS WEREN'T CHARACTERS CREATED IN MY MIND, BUT A RACE AND PEOPLE I HAD COME TO RESPECT AND ADMIRE.
AND AS I LAID THERE BLOODIED AND GROGGY, I COULDN'T HELP BUT CONCERN MYSELF WITH THE SAFETY OF ONE EBEN IN PARTICULAR.

GRAB YOUR HEAVY MACHINERY, LADIES AND GENTLEMEN!
I WANT GROUND SUPPORT FOR THE EBENS AND I WANT IT FIVE MINUTES AGO!
WE RUSHED FROM THE DAMAGED HUT JUST AS THE ATTACKING SWARM FIRED ON THE TINY VILLAGE.

AN IMMENSELY BRIGHT BEAM OF LIGHT HIT THE ALREADY DAMAGED LAB, COLLAPSING A LARGE PORTION OF THE BUILDING'S STRUCTURE.
I WATCHED AS A NUMBER OF EBENS WERE CRUSHED BY DEBRIS.
THERE WAS NOTHING I COULD DO TO SAVE THEM.
AND SUDDENLY THE CONDITIONS ESCALATED.
A MONSTROSITY EMERGED FROM THE LAB, ONLY TO BE FLANKED BY TWO MEMBERS OF THE EBEN MILITARY.
THEY WERE DEAD IN SECONDS.

S EBE2 ATTEMPTED TO HELP THE WOUNDED,
HE CREATURE PINNED HER AGAINST A WALL.
HEARD HER SCREAM.
NOOOOOOOOOOO!
MY SOLDIER INSTINCTS TOOK OVER, AND BEFORE I KNEW IT, I WAS RISKING MY LIFE TO SAVE AN EBEN.

CHAPTER THREE

THE EBENS STOOD IN FEAR AND WATCHED THE CREATURE CORNER ONE OF THEIR OWN.
THIS LAB-MADE MONSTER WAS DANGEROUS AND UNPREDICTABLE. SOMEONE HAD TO STOP IT.
AS I STEPPED TOWARDS THE BEAST, AN EBEN DOCTOR TRIED TO STOP ME FROM WHAT HE CALLED A "CERTAIN DIE," BUT I COULDN'T JUST STAND BY AND WATCH.
I DID WHAT A GOOD SOLDIER WAS TRAINED TO DO... I PUT MY OWN NECK ON THE LINE TO HELP THE INNOCENT.
EBE2 WAS IN MY LINE OF FIRE, SO WITHOUT THINKING, I REMOVED MY KNIFE FROM ITS SHEATH AND SPRINTED TOWARDS THE CREATURE, ARTICULATING MY PLAN OF ATTACK AS I WENT ALONG.
I DISTRACTED IT ENOUGH TO GET IN BETWEEN THE CREATURE AND EBE2, BUT FOR ALL OF THE TRAINING I RECEIVED BACK AT HOME, I FAILED TO ANTICIPATE SUCH A LARGE ANIMAL WAS CAPABLE OF REACTING SO QUICKLY.
IT LUNGED TOWARDS THE TWO OF US AND I SOMEHOW MANAGED TO INTERCEPT WHAT WOULD HAVE BEEN A FATAL BLOW TO EBE2'S HEAD.
BEFORE I KNEW IT, ALIEN CLAWS WERE CUTTING DEEPLY INTO HUMAN FLESH.
MY FLESH.

PAIN WAS NOT AN OPTION FOR ME IN THAT MOMENT. I NEVER ONCE HESITATED, INSTEAD USING THE MONSTER'S ATTACK TO COUNTER.
WITHIN SECONDS I WAS ON ITS BACK, CLAWING MY WAY TOWARDS ITS OVERSIZED SKULL.
BLOOD POURED FROM THE GASH IN MY ARM, BUT IT DID LITTLE TO SLOW ME DOWN.
IN THAT MOMENT NOTHING MATTERED TO ME EXCEPT STOPPING THE BEAST.
AFTER REACHING ITS HEAD, I WASTED NO TIME DRIVING MY BLADE INTO IT.
AS MY PRIMITIVE HUMAN WEAPON CUT DEEPLY INTO ALIEN FLESH, THE BEAST LET OUT A BLOODCURDLING SHRILL.
IT'S A SOUND I'LL NEVER FORGET.
REEEEEEEEEEEEEEEK!
KNOWING EBE2'S BONES WERE FAR MORE FRAGILE AND BRITTLE THAN MY OWN, I LEAPT TO THE GROUND...
JUST IN TIME TO SAVE EBE2 FROM BEING CRUSHED BENEATH THE CREATURE'S LIFELESS BODY.

YOU...
YOU...

DON'T.
ARE YOU OKAY?
I NOT HURT, BUT YOU IS?
I'LL BE FINE.

HE INSIST YOU LET SEE TO WOUND. SAYS HE OWES THAT TO YOU.

IT'S COMPLETELY HEALED!
BUT HOW?
OUR SCIENCE ADVANCEMENTS ARE NOT FOR ONLY MILITARY DEFENSE.

IT'S ABSOLUTELY AMAZING!
IT'S OVER?
THEY'RE RETREATING!

OUR MILITARY HAS FORCED ENEMY TO BE LEAVING.
VICTORY COMES WITH CASUALTY.

THERE'S SO MANY.

TOO MANY.

THE EBENS GATHERED AROUND US, EACH OF THEM WIDE-EYED AND UNCOMMUNICATIVE.
SOME WERE INJURED DURING THE BATTLE, PARTS AND PIECES SEVERED IN THE SURPRISING ONSLAUGHT.
OTHERS WERE NOT SO LUCKY.
HE IS GRATEFUL FOR SAVING LIFE OF ME. HE SAYS YOU SHOW MANY COURAGE.
HE WAS WRONG TO JUDGE. YOUR TEAM NO LONGER LEAVE VILLAGE.
PLEASE TELL YOUR LEADER WE ARE HONORED TO STAY.
YOU... BE... WELCOMED... TO... STAY.
AND TO ALL OF OUR SURPRISE, THE EBEN LEADER SPOKE ENGLISH, AND IN THE PROCESS, SECURED THE SUCCESS OF THE MISSION MOVING FORWARD.

DECEMBER 3, 1967
TODAY WE EXPERIENCED OUR SADDEST DAY TO DATE ON SERPO AS WE ATTENDED A FUNERAL FOR THE EBENS WHO FELL DURING BATTLE.
THE SORROW IN THE EYES OF THE SURVIVING EBENS WILL STAY WITH ME FOREVER.
THE BODIES WERE EACH COVERED IN A TYPE OF WHITE CLOTH, AND ALTHOUGH THEIR FACES WERE HIDDEN FROM US, IT DIDN'T MAKE THE EXPERIENCE ANY LESS EMOTIONAL.
BEFORE THEY WERE PLACED IN METAL CONTAINERS AND BURIED IN A REMOTE LOCATION AWAY FROM THE VILLAGE, THE EBEN LEADER POURED A CEREMONIAL LIQUID OVER EACH BODY AS THE EBENS CHANTED.
THE FUNERAL LASTED FOR A VERY LONG TIME AND WAS TAXING FOR EACH OF US EMOTIONALLY.
BY THE END OF THE DAY, WE ALL HAD A NEWFOUND UNDERSTANDING FOR THE RESPECT THE EBEN PEOPLE HAVE FOR LIFE.

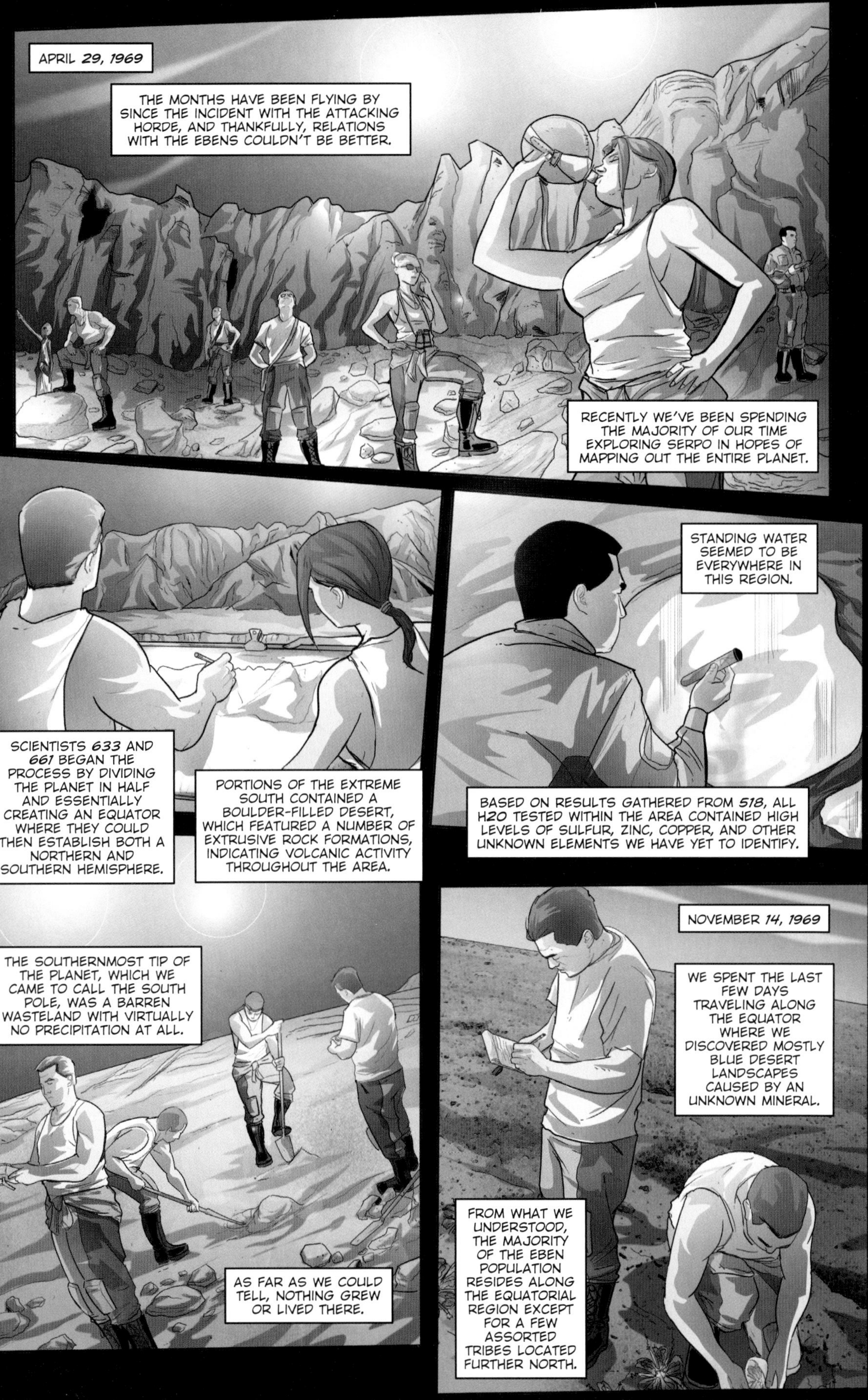
APRIL 29, 1969
THE MONTHS HAVE BEEN FLYING BY SINCE THE INCIDENT WITH THE ATTACKING HORDE, AND THANKFULLY, RELATIONS WITH THE EBENS COULDN'T BE BETTER.
RECENTLY WE'VE BEEN SPENDING THE MAJORITY OF OUR TIME EXPLORING SERPO IN HOPES OF MAPPING OUT THE ENTIRE PLANET.
SCIENTISTS 633 AND 661 BEGAN THE PROCESS BY DIVIDING THE PLANET IN HALF AND ESSENTIALLY CREATING AN EQUATOR WHERE THEY COULD THEN ESTABLISH BOTH A NORTHERN AND SOUTHERN HEMISPHERE.
PORTIONS OF THE EXTREME SOUTH CONTAINED A BOULDER-FILLED DESERT, WHICH FEATURED A NUMBER OF EXTRUSIVE ROCK FORMATIONS, INDICATING VOLCANIC ACTIVITY THROUGHOUT THE AREA.
STANDING WATER SEEMED TO BE EVERYWHERE IN THIS REGION.
BASED ON RESULTS GATHERED FROM 518, ALL H2O TESTED WITHIN THE AREA CONTAINED HIGH LEVELS OF SULFUR, ZINC, COPPER, AND OTHER UNKNOWN ELEMENTS WE HAVE YET TO IDENTIFY.
THE SOUTHERNMOST TIP OF THE PLANET, WHICH WE CAME TO CALL THE SOUTH POLE, WAS A BARREN WASTELAND WITH VIRTUALLY NO PRECIPITATION AT ALL.
AS FAR AS WE COULD TELL, NOTHING GREW OR LIVED THERE.
NOVEMBER 14, 1969
WE SPENT THE LAST FEW DAYS TRAVELING ALONG THE EQUATOR WHERE WE DISCOVERED MOSTLY BLUE DESERT LANDSCAPES CAUSED BY AN UNKNOWN MINERAL.
FROM WHAT WE UNDERSTOOD, THE MAJORITY OF THE EBEN POPULATION RESIDES ALONG THE EQUATORIAL REGION EXCEPT FOR A FEW ASSORTED TRIBES LOCATED FURTHER NORTH.

IT WAS HERE THAT THE TEAM FOUND POCKETS OF FRESH WATER FED BY ARTESIAN WELLS.
BASED ON PERSONAL EXPERIENCE ALONE I CAN SAY THAT THE WATER TASTED NORMAL, THOUGH IT WAS DECIDED WE WOULD NOT DRINK IT BECAUSE OF UNKNOWN BACTERIA DISCOVERED DURING RANDOM CULTURE TESTS.
DECEMBER 26, 1969
WE CELEBRATED CHRISTMAS YESTERDAY EVEN THOUGH WE CAN'T BE SURE IF WE HAVE THE RIGHT DATE. IT WAS FITTING CONSIDERING THE TEAM SPENT THE LAST HALF A WEEK EXPLORING A TOWERING EVERGREEN-TYPE FOREST IN THE NORTHERN HEMISPHERE.
NEEDLESS TO SAY THERE WAS A MAJOR CLIMATE DIFFERENCE HERE AS MILLIONS OF OVERSIZED CHRISTMAS TREES GREW TO IMPRESSIVE HEIGHTS AROUND US.
225 DECIDED TO CALL IT "LITTLE MONTANA" ON ACCOUNT OF IT REMINDING HIM OF HOME IN AN ODD AND ALMOST SURREAL SORT OF WAY.
IT'S HERE WHERE WE WITNESSED THE EBENS MILK THE WHITE FLUID WE'VE BEEN DRINKING FROM THE TREES, WHICH TO MY UNDERSTANDING THEY INGEST FOR NUTRITIONAL PURPOSES.
ANOTHER SOURCE OF EBEN FOOD CAME FROM THIS REGION AS WELL.
A BULBOUS PLANT GREW IN THE MARSHES ON THE OUTSKIRTS OF THE FOREST, WHICH EBE2 CONTINUOUSLY REFERRED TO AS "SNACKS."
AFTER TRYING THEM FIRSTHAND, I CAN SAY THAT THEY TASTED SIMILAR TO A MELON, THOUGH THEY HAD A DIFFERENT CONSISTENCY THAN WHAT YOU'D EXPECT.
RADIATION LEVELS WERE LOWEST IN THE NORTHERN REGION, AS WERE THE TEMPERATURES.

IN FACT, THE NORTH POLE REGISTERED A CONSTANT 33 DEGREES FAHRENHEIT THROUGHOUT THE DAY.
IT SNOWED FREQUENTLY THERE, BUT NOT WHITE FLAKES OF FLUFFY PRECIPITATION.
NO, SNOW AS THE EBENS KNEW IT WAS A GREEN, CRYSTALLIZED MIX OF WATER AND UNIDENTIFIED ELEMENTS THAT SEEMED TO BURN WHEN IT CAME IN CONTACT WITH OUR SKIN.
CONFIRMING WHAT WE WERE TAUGHT BACK AT CAMP PERRY THROUGHOUT OUR EBEN ANATOMY TRAINING, THE PEOPLE OF SERPO SUFFERED FROM A HEIGHTENED FORM OF HYPOTHERMIA WHEN EXPOSED TO EXTREME LOW TEMPERATURES.
IT WAS FOR THIS EXACT REASON THAT WE CAME EQUIPPED WITH LIQUID NITROGEN TANKS ON THE MISSION SHOULD THE EBENS EVER BECOME HOSTILE.
BUT LIKE OUR HANDGUNS, I'VE COME TO LEARN WE'LL HAVE NO REASON TO USE THE NITROGEN.
WHY DO YOU KEEP SERPO IN CONTAINERS?
WE HAVE MANY SCIENTISTS ON EARTH WHO WILL BE WAITING TEN YEARS TO SEE THE WONDERS OF YOUR PLANET.
OUR JOURNEY HERE IS THE GREATEST DISCOVERY IN THE HISTORY OF MY PEOPLE AND THEY'RE GOING TO HAVE A LOT OF QUESTIONS WHEN WE RETURN.
HOPEFULLY THESE SAMPLES WILL ANSWER A FEW OF THEM.
DO YOU LIKE SERPO?
I MISS HOME FROM TIME TO TIME, BUT KEEPING BUSY IS MY MEDICINE.
AND I HAVE TO ADMIT, YOU'VE DONE A PRETTY GOOD JOB AT KEEPING ME COMPANY.
SO I AM SUITABLE EARTH FRIEND?
LET'S JUST SAY THAT YOU'VE BEEN A PLEASANT SURPRISE.

OCTOBER 1, 1973
TIME CONTINUES TO TICK AWAY AS WE WORK TOWARDS COMPLETING EACH OF OUR MISSION'S OBJECTIVES.
LATELY OUR FOCUS HAS BEEN ON THE ANIMAL LIFE, WHICH FOR MUCH OF THE TEAM, HAS BEEN A REFRESHING CHANGE OF PACE.
WE FIRST EXAMINED A CREATURE THAT WAS A HYBRID OF AN ARMADILLO AND A MANGY CAT.
UNFORTUNATELY, THE ALIEN MAMMAL WAS EXTREMELY HOSTILE. EVERY TIME THE TEAM WOULD ATTEMPT TO INSPECT IT, IT WOULD CHASE US AWAY, HISSING AND SPITTING.
EBE2 SEEMED TO FIND THIS VERY AMUSING.
THE BEAST, AS 518 COINED IT, WAS A MASSIVE OX-LIKE ANIMAL.
AS FRIGHTENING AS THE CREATURE LOOKED, IT WAS ACTUALLY DOCILE AND TIMID.
420 EVEN JOKED ABOUT TAKING ONE HOME AND SETTING IT UP ON HIS FAMILY FARM.
IN THE MOUNTAINOUS DESERT TO THE SOUTH, A LION-LIKE CREATURE... HAIRLESS EXCEPT FOR A PATCH OF LONG FUR AROUND ITS NECK... WAS ABUNDANT.
LIKE 518'S BEAST, IT TOO WAS HARMLESS, AND AT TIMES, COULD EVEN BE DESCRIBED AS FRIENDLY.
FISH WERE NON-EXISTENT ON SERPO, THOUGH BODIES OF WATER ALONG THE EQUATOR DID CONTAIN ODD LOOKING EEL-LIKE CREATURES THAT MEASURED OUT TO ABOUT FORTY INCHES IN LENGTH.

WHILE TRUDGING THROUGH AN OASIS IN THE SOUTHERN HEMISPHERE, A SIMILAR LAND-BASED CREATURE WAS DISCOVERED BY THE TEAM, THOUGH UNLIKE ITS WATER-BASED COUSIN, THIS ODDITY'S EYES WERE STRANGELY HUMAN IN APPEARANCE.
THE SNAKE MONSTER ATTACKED WITHOUT PROVOCATION, PINNING 633 AGAINST A ROCK AND STRIKING.
IT BIT HER IN THE THIGH BEFORE WE COULD INTERVENE, BUT THANKFULLY THE WOUND WASN'T LIFE THREATENING.
UNFORTUNATELY THE CREATURE'S SECOND ATTACK WOULD PROVE FATAL, THOUGH NOT FOR OUR SCIENTIST.
AS 899 ATTEMPTED TO DISTRACT IT, I PULLED 633 TO SAFETY.
BUT IN THE PROCESS, 899 WAS LEFT DEFENSELESS.

ALTHOUGH IT WAS AGAINST THE RULES OF THE EBEN PEOPLE TO KILL ANIMALS OF SERPO, I ORDERED MY MEN TO USE LETHAL FORCE IMMEDIATELY.
WE FIRED ON THE CREATURE, UNLOADING ROUND AFTER ROUND INTO IT.
AND WHEN THE DUST SETTLED, TWO LIFELESS BODIES WERE SPRAWLED OUT ON THE GROUND.
ONE OF THEM BEING 899.
THERE'S BEEN AN ACCIDENT. PLEASE!
CAN YOU HELP! IS THERE SOMETHING YOU CAN DO?
ALTHOUGH THERE WAS NO PULSE TO BE FOUND, WE DIDN'T WANT TO GIVE UP HOPE FOR 899... AND NEITHER DID THE EBENS.
THE EBEN LEADER ORDERED THAT 899'S BODY BE TAKEN TO THE LAB.
THE EBENS TRIED EVERYTHING TO REVIVE 899, BUT DEATH IS INCURABLE. A VERY BENEVOLENT AND CARING PEOPLE, THEY INSTANTLY SAW THE SADNESS IN THE TEAM AND TRIED TO COMFORT US IN THEIR OWN WAY.
I HAVE SO MUCH RESPECT FOR THEM... AND NOW, SO DOES 203.
THE TEAM HELD A BURIAL SERVICE FOR 899 JUST A FEW HOURS AGO.
ALMOST THE ENTIRE VILLAGE ATTENDED THE CEREMONY, WHICH WAS LED BY 420 AS HE ACTED IN THE ROLE OF A MINISTER.
IT WAS AN EMOTIONAL MOMENT FOR US ALL, BUT IN RETROSPECT, WE CAN'T HELP BUT BE ETERNALLY GRATEFUL TO THE EBENS FOR THEIR CARING AND SYMPATHETIC ATTITUDE TOWARDS THE LOSS OF OUR FRIEND AND FELLOW SOLDIER.
R.I.P. 899
I'M SADDENED TO THINK THAT HE'LL NEVER SEE HOME AGAIN, BUT AT THE SAME TIME, 899 LOVED SERPO SO MUCH THAT I'M SURE HE'S HONORED TO HAVE ITS SOIL AS HIS FINAL RESTING PLACE.
WE WILL NEVER FORGET HIM.

JANUARY 20, 1978
I CALLED A MANDATORY MEETING EARLIER TODAY TO DISCUSS PROTOCOL FOR THE TEAM'S DEPARTURE FROM SERPO, AS WELL AS TO GAUGE EVERYONE'S EMOTIONAL HANDLING OF THE SITUATION.
AFTER ALL, WE'VE SPENT THE LAST DECADE HERE, AND IN MANY WAYS, IT HAS BECOME OUR HOME AWAY FROM HOME.
I KNOW THIS HAS BEEN A LONG, AND TRYING MISSION, BUT WE'RE ABOUT TO MAKE OUR WAY HOME. I NEED TO BE SURE THAT EVERY ONE OF YOU IS PREPARED FOR NOT ONLY OUR JOURNEY BACK, BUT WHAT TO EXPECT WHEN WE GET THERE.
I'M SURE WE'LL BE DEBRIEFED ON WHAT TO SAY TO THE PRESS, BUT WHATEVER IT IS YOU DECIDE TO TELL, MAKE SURE YOU CHOOSE YOUR WORDS WISELY. THEY WILL HAVE A LASTING IMPACT ON PEOPLE WHO MAY NOT BE READY TO GRASP WHAT WE'VE BEEN INVOLVED IN.
THERE'S JUST NO GETTING AROUND THAT.
ALSO, WE CAN'T FORGET WHAT HAPPENED TO 308 ON OUR WAY HERE. ON OUR RETURN FLIGHT, WE FOLLOW ALL INSTRUCTIONS OF THE EBEN PILOTS.
I WANT ALL TEN OF US GETTING HOME SAFELY.
WHAT WOULD YOU THINK IF ONLY NINE WENT BACK?
WHAT DO YOU MEAN, 661?
I'D LIKE PERMISSION TO STAY ON SERPO TO CONTINUE MY RESEARCH AND, ULTIMATELY, LIVE AMONGST ITS PEOPLE.
THERE MAY NOT BE ANY OTHERS WHO COME HERE. ARE YOU PREPARED FOR THAT?
I'M FULLY AWARE OF THE CONSEQUENCES OF MY DECISION.
I'M PREPARED TO LIVE OUT THE REMAINDER OF MY DAYS HERE.
MAKE THAT EIGHT GOING HOME.
I'D LIKE TO FORMALLY PUT IN MY REQUEST TO STAY ON SERPO AS WELL.

YOU?

I MADE AN ASS OUT OF MYSELF WITH THE WAY I ACTED. I'LL BE THE FIRST TO ADMIT THAT. I WAS SCARED AND I LASHED OUT, BLAMING SERPO AND ITS PEOPLE FOR EVERYTHING THAT WENT WRONG.
BUT THAT WAS BEFORE I *OPENED MY EYES*.

IT TOOK SOME TIME, BUT I FINALLY SAW THE UNQUESTIONABLE GOODNESS IN THE PEOPLE HERE, AND IN THE PROCESS, I REALIZED IT WAS ME WHO WAS THE MALICIOUS ONE ALL ALONG.
I OWE THE EBENS A GREAT DEAL, AND IF GIVEN PERMISSION, I'D LIKE TO STAY BEHIND.
THE WAY I SEE IT, I HAVE A LOT MORE TO LEARN, AND YOU NEVER KNOW, MAYBE I COULD TEACH THEM A FEW THINGS ABOUT US ALONG THE WAY, TOO.

PERMISSION GRANTED.

JANUARY 22, 1978
WE'RE SCHEDULED TO LEAVE TOMORROW AND SAYING GOOD-BYE TO SERPO IS PROVING MORE DIFFICULT THAN I ORIGINALLY THOUGHT.
AS I WRITE THIS, I CAN'T ESCAPE THE UNWANTED UNDERSTANDING THAT THERE ARE SOME PIECES OF THIS PLACE THAT I WISH I DIDN'T HAVE TO GIVE UP.... THE PEOPLE, THEIR NATURE, AND MORE THAN ANYTHING, THEIR WAY OF LIFE.

YOU MUST BE EXCITED TO RETURN.
I AM, BUT NOT AS MUCH AS I THOUGHT I'D BE.

WHAT YOU MEAN?
A PART OF ME WISHES I DIDN'T HAVE TO LEAVE. I'VE GROWN TO LOVE AND RESPECT YOUR PEOPLE AND THIS PLANET AND I'M A BIT UNSURE OF WHAT IS WAITING FOR ME BACK ON EARTH.
I LOVE MY COUNTRY, BUT IT'S BY NO MEANS PERFECT. THERE'S A LOT WRONG THERE, AND MORE THAN THAT, THERE'S A LOT OF PAIN WE BRING TO EACH OTHER. IT'S SOMETHING I HAVEN'T SEEN HERE AT ALL. I'M NOT SURE IF I'M RETURNING HOME... OR LEAVING IT.

I SPENT MY ENTIRE LIFE THINKING I KNEW ALL OF THE ANSWERS, BUT IT TOOK ME TRAVELING A MILLION LIGHT YEARS TO REALIZE WHAT IT MEANS TO BE HUMAN... AND TO MY SURPRISE... WHAT IT MEANS TO BE EBEN.

ALL THIS TIME YET I STILL NOT KNOWING YOUR NAME.

NOW YOU DO.

THANK YOU.

NO... THANK YOU.
FOR EVERYTHING!

I NEVER THOUGHT I'D BE DREADING THE DAY I'D RETURN TO MY OWN PLANET.
I'VE UNKNOWINGLY FALLEN FOR SO MUCH OF WHAT SERPO HAS TO OFFER THAT I FIND MYSELF WANTING TO STAY WITH 661 AND 203.
BUT I KNOW HOW IMPORTANT IT IS TO SHARE EVERYTHING WE'VE DISCOVERED WITH THE PEOPLE OF EARTH... AND I HOPE THAT IN DOING SO, IT WILL MAKE US A BETTER SOCIETY AND THAT WE CAN LEARN BY EXAMPLE.

JANUARY 23, 1978
THE DAY WE LEFT SERPO FOREVER.
NOT MUCH WAS SAID.
AFTER ALL, THEY SAY "ACTIONS SPEAK LOUDER THAN WORDS."
IN MANY WAYS, I ENVIED THOSE WHO STAYED BEHIND.
ESPECIALLY WHEN THINKING ABOUT ALL THAT I'D BE LOSING.
BUT AS COMMANDER OF THIS DECADE-LONG OPERATION, THE MISSION WILL NOT BE DEEMED COMPLETE UNTIL I STEP FOOT ON AMERICAN SOIL.
AND THAT LEAVES ME WITH NO CHOICE BUT TO RETURN HOME...
REGARDLESS OF HOW DIFFICULT THE TRANSITION WILL BE.

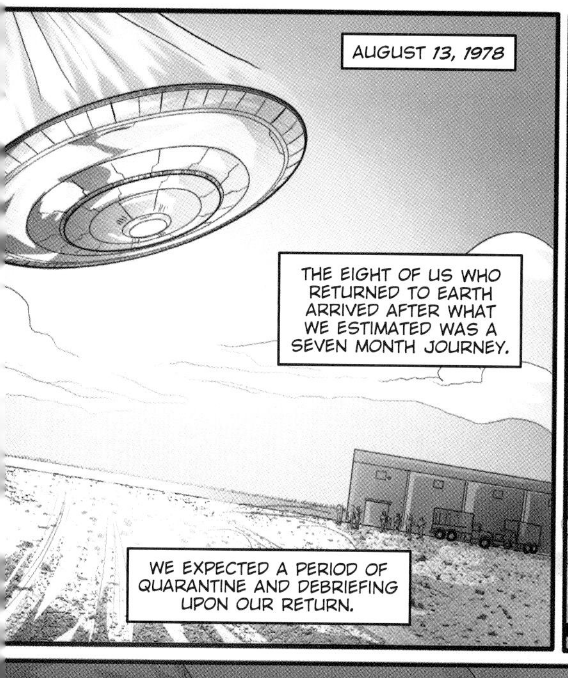
AUGUST 13, 1978
THE EIGHT OF US WHO RETURNED TO EARTH ARRIVED AFTER WHAT WE ESTIMATED WAS A SEVEN MONTH JOURNEY.
WE EXPECTED A PERIOD OF QUARANTINE AND DEBRIEFING UPON OUR RETURN.

PRIOR TO TOUCHING DOWN, WE DISCUSSED HOW EXCITING IT WOULD BE TO STEP OUT INTO THE WELCOMING PARTY OF PRESS, MILITARY AND SPECTATORS.
INSTEAD WE WERE ESCORTED OFF OF THE SHIP AND IMMEDIATELY LOADED INTO THE BACK OF A TRUCK.

WE WERE NOT CONTACTED BY ANYONE DURING THE LONG JOURNEY FROM THE LANDING SITE TO AN UNDISCLOSED LOCATION.

PON ARRIVAL TO THE NAMELESS BASE, E TEAM WAS IMMEDIATELY IMPRISONED AND ISOLATED FROM NOT ONLY EACH THER, BUT THE REST OF THE WORLD.
AT'S WHEN I KNEW THERE WOULD BE NO PRESS WAITING TO HEAR OUR TORY. NO CELEBRATION. NO SHARING OF THE WONDERS WE LEARNED ROM A DISTANT GALAXY.
WE WERE TOLD IF WE COOPERATED, WE'D BE GIVEN NEW IDENTITIES ND COULD EVENTUALLY SSIMILATE BACK INTO SOCIETY, SO LONG AS VE NEVER DISCUSSED YTHING PERTAINING TO ROJECT SERPO AGAIN.
EVERYTHING I BELIEVED IN HAD CHANGED. EVERYTHING I HELD DEAR WAS GONE.

AND AS A FITTING END TO THE NIGHTMARE I WAS NOW LIVING, I CAME ACROSS THE TELLING SCRIBBLING OF THE EBEN WHO RESIDED IN THE CELL BEFORE ME.
"HUMANS KNOW NOT APPRECIATION FOR LIFE."

LUXOPLEX
THEATER CLOSED
KEEP OUT

THIS IS *UNBELIEVABLE*. HOW CAN IT BE TRUE?
BUT AT THE SAME TIME... HOW CAN IT NOT?
AND THOSE GUYS AT THE MOTEL... WHY WOULD THEY WANT TO KILL OVER SOME *MADE-UP STORY*?

ALL I KNOW IS... THIS HAS BEEN KEPT UNDER WRAPS FOR TOO LONG. I'VE GOT TO GET THIS TO FRED.

WHAT THE HELL?

SON OF A BITCH!
ARGH!
PFT
SHIT!
PFT
PFT
PFT
PFT

I CAN'T JUST LEAVE IT.
BUT I'M NOT GOING TO GET ***KILLED*** OVER IT EITHER.

PFT
PFT
PFT
PFT
PFT
PFT

UGH!
PFT
THUD!
SON OF A BITCH! THE DIARY... I'VE GOT NOTHING. I'VE GOT ABSOLUTELY NO STORY WHATSOEVER!

WAIT!
THE OLD MAN!

MEMORIAL HOSPITAL

YOU WEREN'T EASY TO FIND, OLD MAN, BUT *12* YEARS AS A BEAT REPORTER HAS ITS BENEFITS.

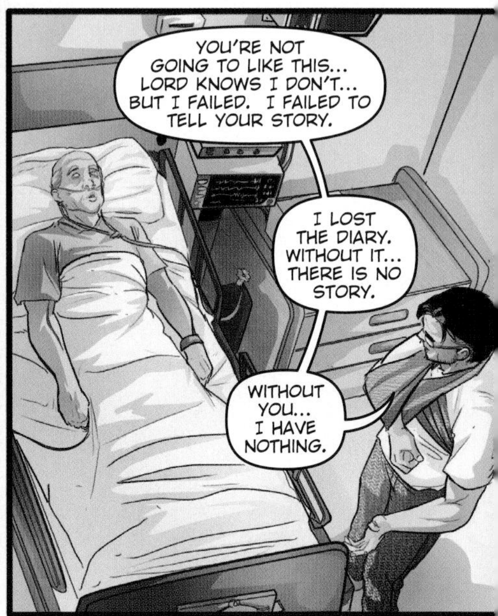
YOU'RE NOT GOING TO LIKE THIS... LORD KNOWS I DON'T... BUT I FAILED. I FAILED TO TELL YOUR STORY.
I LOST THE DIARY. WITHOUT IT... THERE IS NO STORY.
WITHOUT YOU... I HAVE NOTHING.

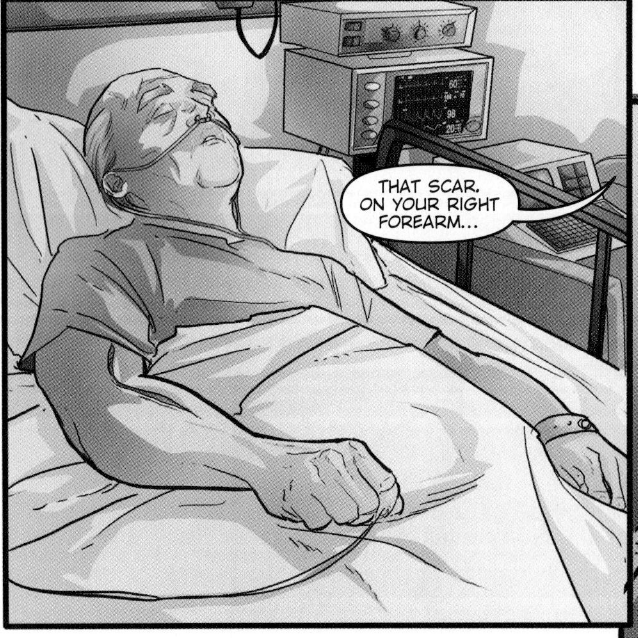
THAT SCAR. ON YOUR RIGHT FOREARM...

YOU'RE HIM! YOU'RE COMMANDER 102.

THERE'S... *THERE'S ANOTHER!*

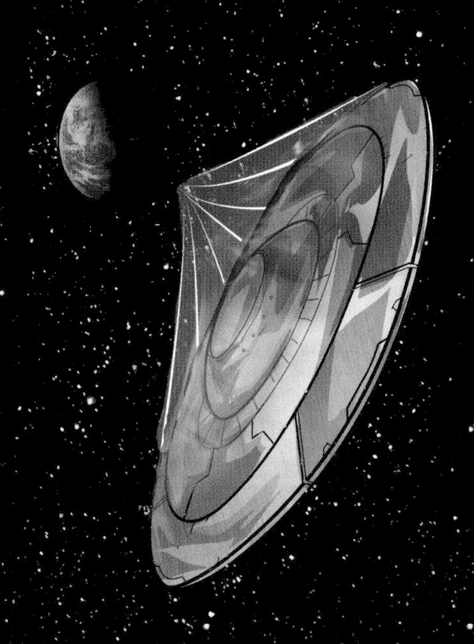

Project Serpo

COSMIC TOP SECRET
EYES ONLY

BRIEFING DOCUMENT: PROJECT SERPO
PREPARED ON 05 FEBRUARY, 1979

WARNING: This is a COSMIC TOP SECRET - EYES ONLY document containing compartmentalized information essential to the national security of the United States. EYES ONLY ACCESS to the material herein is strictly limited to those possessing COSMIC Top Secret clearance level. Reproduction in any form or the taking of written or mechanically transcribed notes is strictly forbidden.

Title: Senior Officer Debriefing Report: Project Serpo

Distribution Statement: Cosmic Top Secret

Report Date: 05 February, 1979

Document Number: 80HQD893-020

Background

This debriefing report covers the logistical details surrounding the acclaimed crash at Roswell, New Mexico in July of 1947, as well the interplanetary exchange program that later followed.

Regardless of what has been refuted by the United States government, a crash at Roswell, New Mexico in July 1942 involving extraterrestrial aircraft did in fact occur. There were two crash sites - one located southwest of Corona, NM and a second at Pelona Peak, NM. An archaeology team discovered the Corona wreckage shortly after the crash where one live entity was found hiding behind a rock. It came to be known as EBEI (Extraterrestrial Biological Entity) and remained in a living capacity until 1952.

While in captivity, rudimentary communication was established. EBEI provided the location of its home planet and explanations of devices recovered from the crash. One such item was a communication device, which EBEI used to contact its planet of origin in the Zeta Reticular star system known as Serpo.

Several signals were sent to Serpo during the summer of 1952. In early fall, a response was received. In total, six messages were sent:

- The first was to let its home planet know he was alive;
- The second explained the crash in 1947 and the death of the crew;
- The third requested an Eben rescue craft;
- The fourth suggested a formal meeting with leaders of Earth;
- The fifth suggested an exchange program;
- The sixth provided landing coordinates for future rescue or visitation to Earth.

While the EBEI was alive, it assisted with translating the Eben transmissions, though only about 30% of them were deciphered. Following EBEI's death in 1952, a team of linguist specialists from various U.S. and foreign universities were called in to aide in the translation. Since the translations were going poorly, we sent messages to the Ebens in English. Months later a reply was received in broken English.

The messages became clearer, but not clear enough. It became extremely difficult to coordinate a date, time, and location for an Eben landing on Earth. Things were further complicated by the Ebens having a different time and date system than ours.

It took several years to perfect and understand the Eben language. The language barrier resulted in a tried and failed attempt during April 1964 in the southern sector of White Sands Missile Range, New Mexico. However, a new target date and location was decided on – July of 1965 at a highly secure Nevada atomic test site.

Preparing for an Intergalactic Exchange

With a second landing scheduled, the US Air Force was tasked to lead in the planning and crew selection. It was decided that each crew member would be career military, single with no children, and have special cross-trained skills. Sixteen candidates were selected from 56,000 files that were screened. This allowed for the top twelve to make the journey with four replacements standing by. Of the I2 selected (I0 male, 2 female), 8 were US Air Force, 2 US Army, and 2 U.S. Navy. The group came to be known simply as the Team Members.

All Team Members were thoroughly 'sheep-dipped' - erased from their military roles and wiped from the system. Records purged included: Social Security, Internal Revenue, medical and military, as well as any other identification that could tie the members to the program. It was suggested they be classified as Dead , but ultimately they became listed as Missing on official records, and Discharged on unofficial records.

Once Team Members were indoctrinated in the program, they were no longer identified by name and given instead a three-digit number. From that point on, they were known and referred to only by a number. They were never to use their real names again once they left Earth, and the Team was disciplined enough to continue using their three-digit numbers on Serpo. The Team composition was as follows:

Team Commander - I02
Assistant Team Commander - 203
Team Pilot #I - 225
Team Pilot #2 - 308
Linguist #I - 420
Linguist #2 - 475
Biologist - 5I8
Scientist #I - 633
Scientist #2 - 66I
Doctor #I - 700
Doctor #2 - 754
Security - 899

Training took place at closely guarded training facilities in Camp Perry, VA, Sheppard AFB, TX; Ellsworth AFB, SD; Dow AFB, MN; and isolated locations in Mexico and Chile. Team Members went through extensive exercises to demonstrate their abilities to endure hardship, both physically and mentally. A battery of tests, screenings, and training were conducted some of which included:

- Introduction to Space Exploration, Astronomy, and Astrophysics;
- Eben Anthropology and Eben History (basic information received from EBEI);
- Weightless and Zero Oxygen Environment Training;
- Survival, Escape and Evasion Training;
- Basic Weapons and Explosive Training (6 pounds of C-4 was taken);
- Psychological Operations Training and Anti-Interrogation Preparation;
- Physical Stress Training;
- Methods to cope with Confinement/Isolation;
- Basic Biology;

Each Team Member was given the standard 'pill' issued to intelligence agents operating behind enemy lines. The pill could end their life if, for some reason, the Ebens turned out to be hostile. Selected Members were also given small containers of liquid nitrogen after EBEI informed intelligence officers that the Eben people were vulnerable to extreme cold. This would aid the team in neutralizing the Ebens should an escape be necessary.

Countless hours went into the planning of the Serpo mission with debate and discussions on what equipment and supplies to send for every conceivable situation. Sixteen different types of cameras were sent so Team Members could capture the look and makeup of Serpo objects, artifacts, and landscapes.

There were two planned locations - one a "cover" location at Holloman Air Force Base, and the other being the actual location near the southern entrance to White Sands Army Post. To prevent Team Members from communicating with anyone from the outside world, they were transported to the Disciplinary Barracks at Ft. Leavenworth, Kansas, where they were confined in locked cells. They remained there under close watch until the exchange.

In July of 1965, the Eben craft entered our atmosphere and landed at the Nevada Test site. A mix of senior political and military officials greeted the alien visitors as they exited their craft and walked under a pre-constructed canopy. Communication was in English. The Ebens brought electronic translating devices to facilitate communications, which they later left with military officials as a gift of good faith.

The remains of eleven dead alien bodies from prior crashes were presented to the Ebens and taken on board, along with the 12 Team Members, and 16 pallets of equipment and supplies weighing approximately 4 tons.

The Journey to Serpo

It took the Team nine months to travel the distance from Earth to Serpo in the Eben craft. Team Members described the alien craft in their diaries as containing three separate levels. Their cargo was stored in the lower level, Team Members remained in the middle level, while the Eben crew was on the upper level. There were no windows. About six hours into the trip, they intercepted and transferred to an extremely large craft for the remainder of the deep space journey.

The Team Members experienced space sickness that included dizziness, blurred vision, nausea, confusion, and disorientation. They were isolated in bubble like spheres. While in the spheres, they lost track of time. All their instruments to record time did not work properly.

Problems were encountered with waste since there were no bathroom facilities. Their space sickness intensified during what was estimated to be one month into the trip. The Ebens gave them a milky liquid and pointed a bluish light on their heads that seemed to reduce the sickness.

At one point late in the journey, an Eben arrived and motioned the Team to leave the spheres. After walking for about 20 minutes within the enormous craft, they were taken into an elevator type device and brought to what they believed was the control room. Many Ebens were seated at four different stations containing control and instrument panels with many lights. They were able to identify many television screens displaying Eben language along with vertical and horizontal lines.

The Team was given permission to wander around the ship with the provision they remain together. 633 wanted to see the engines. The group was taken to a room containing very large metal containers arranged in a circular pattern. At the center was a copper colored coil with a bright light shining through the coil s center from above.

After awakening from a long time in the space sphere, the Team realized that one Team Member was not with them - number 308. They are told that "308 is not living". The Team was in a state of confusion and 308's death only worsened the situation. The Eben crew would not allow the Team to remove 308 from his sphere to examine his body for fear of infection. They decided to wait until arriving on the planet to investigate his death further.

When they finally arrived on the planet, they were greeted by a large number of Ebens. The largest Eben welcomed them to the planet through a translator. The Team assumed that this large Eben was the leader.

The landscape was desert. There were no hills or vegetation, just dirt. The temperature was 107. The sky was clear, blue and contained two suns. They were brought to the central village containing large electrical tower-like structures. The living quarters resembled adobe or mud huts.

They were introduced to an Eben, who they named Ebe2. Ebe2 spoke almost fluent English and became their guide and translator during their stay on Serpo.

Ebe2 led the Team to a series of adobe style huts with underground storage areas. Their gear was stored at the huts. The igloo looking house was made of a rubberized, concrete like material. There were lights in the ceiling. The Team took inventory of all gear and settled in for their mission.

Planet Serpo Information

Location – Zeta Reticular Star System (binary star system – 2 suns)

Number of planets in Eben Solar System – 6

Age of Serpo – Approximately 3 billion years

Diameter – 7,218 miles (a little less than Earth)

Mass – 5.06×10^{24}

Moons – 2

Surface gravity – 9.60 m/s 2

Rotation Periods – 43 hours

Orbit – 865 days (Serpo orbits only one of the two suns)

Tilt – 43 degrees

Temperature – Min 43° / Max 126°

Atmosphere – Carbon, Hydrogen, Oxygen, Nitrogen

Distance from Earth – 38.43 light years

Nearest planet to Serpo – Otto

Distance – 88 million miles (colonized by Ebens with research base, but no natural inhabitants on Otto)

Nearest inhabited planet to Serpo – Silus (made up of various creatures, but no intelligent life forms. Ebens use the planet to mine minerals.)

Distance – 434 million miles

Geological Information

The planet was estimated to be about three billion years old and its two suns to be about five billion years old. Serpo orbited around only one of the suns, these two together orbited the other sun.

One of the first things the Team did was map the planet. They divided it into different hemispheres, then explored and studied each. The geological make up of Serpo is much different than Earth. There are few mountains, no oceans, and only a scattered handful of plants similar to trees.

The southern pole is a barren desert with virtually no precipitation. Temperatures measured between 90° and 135°F. Absolutely nothing grew in this area.

There s a major change in climate and landscape at the Northern Hemisphere. One Team Member named it "Little Montana" where trees similar to Evergreens grew. The Ebens milked a white fluid from these trees, which they drank. Numerous types of vegetation were found in this region. In one area, marsh lands were found. Large plants were observed growing in the marshy area. The Ebens used these plants for food. The bulb of the plant was very large and tasted something like a melon.

Since much of the planet was uninhabitable, most of the Eben communities were established at the planet s equator. The Ebens lived comfortably in this hot, desert-style landscape. Some patches of vegetation grew, along with numerous pockets of underground water. The water appeared fresh, however our scientists found traces of unknown chemicals and bacteria. Even though the Ebens drank and used it with no apparent harm, our Team boiled it before consuming.

Animal Life

During the Team s exploration, they discovered numerous types of animals, one of which resembled an armadillo. The creature was extremely hostile. On several occasions it tried to attack the Team. The Eben guide used a type of sound device (sonic-directed beam) to drive the creature away.

They observed a strange animal that they called the "Beast", which looked similar to a large Ox. Unlike the armadillo creature, this animal was very timid and never exhibited any hostility.

Another creature appeared that looked like a Mountain Lion, but had long fur around the neck. This animal was curious, but was not considered hostile by the Ebens.

The Team also found a very long (approximately 15 feet) and large creature that resembled a snake. The Ebens warned against this creature explaining to the Team that it was "deadly". The creature s head was large with two eyes that were described as human-like. The creature made threatening maneuvers toward the Team and they killed it with a .45 caliber handgun. It was the only time they used their weapons to killed a creature. The Ebens became upset over this, not that the Team killed the creature, but that they used a weapon.

The Team was permitted to dissect the snake creature. The internal organs were unlike any seen before by our biologists and had no resemblance to an Earth-style snake. Examination of the eyes revealed cones, irises, and large optic nerves similar to that of a human eye. The brain was larger than any Earth-based snake.

Serpo did have some bodies of water, not as large and expansive as an ocean. Within these bodies of water, our Team did not discover any species of fish, however some bodies of water near the equator did contain strange-looking creatures about 8-10" long similar to eels.

They were not able to locate any extensive populations of bird species. During their entire stay on Serpo only two types of flying creatures were observed. There was one that resembled a hawk and another that looked like a large flying squirrel. Team Members were unable to catch either one for examination, but found that neither species was aggressive.

Like the bird population, insects did not appear in large swarms or numbered species. The Team did experience aggravation from small bugs similar to cockroaches, but smaller, that would get into their equipment. They ultimately discovered the bugs to be a harmless nuisance. The cockroach like bug had a hardened shell, with a soft interior body. The Team never observed any flying insects, such as flies, wasps, etc. Several other small bugs were found and identified.

Eben History

The original home of the Eben people was a planet other than Serpo. It was destroyed about 5,000 years ago by extreme volcanic activity. The Ebens were forced to relocate and inhabit Serpo to preserve their species and civilization, estimated to be about 10,000 years old.

The Ebens fought in a great planetary war some 3,000 years ago that lasted about 100 years. The war was between the Ebens and another race and was fought with advanced particle beams developed by both civilizations. Thousands of Ebens were killed during this 100 year war, but eventually they were able to destroy their enemy s planet and kill all remaining enemy forces.

Eben Society

The population of Serpo was estimated at 650,000. They have a family structure similar to Earth with each male having a female mate. Most families were small, never exceeding more than two children. The civilization was very structured, planning even the birth of each and every child to allow proper social grouping of the population.

The Eben society had similar occupations and facilities as ours. There were scientists, doctors, and technicians, as well as education facilities. There was virtually no crime. There were a total of about 100 different villages on Serpo. Most of the planet remained unoccupied. They had developed some sort of electrical power system that our Team was never able to understand. Somehow they were able to tap into a special vacuum and release an enormous amount of energy. This is the same energy source they used to power and propel their spacecraft.

The Eben civilization did not use money. Each Eben was issued what they needed. In place of stores and shopping centers were large, central distribution centers where Ebens would go to obtain items and food of need. Everyone in the Eben civilization worked in some capacity, except for the children. The Eben children matured at an alarming rate compared to Earth children.

Eben Culture & Entertainment

While the Ebens worked long hours compared to us - a typical work day was about 43 hours with only 3 rest periods within that time - they did find time to entertain. Their culture was deep with music and dance. They would listen to a musical instrument that sounded like tonal rhythms and chant sounds that was the Eben equivalent to our singing.

Certain periods were celebrated with a ritual dance in which the Ebens would form a circle and dance around. During the ceremony, music was played on instruments similar to bells and drums.

The one form of a game our Team learned was a team sport played like soccer only with a larger ball. Like soccer, the object was to kick the ball down a field and into a goal. The game lasted for a very long time and had many strange rules our Team found difficult to understand. This game was very popular among the Eben children.

Death also occurred on Serpo. Our Team witnessed Ebens die, some of natural causes, some by accident. Since our Team was unable to judge the age of an Eben and our time measurements did not apply on Serpo. They referred to their lifespan as 'life periods'. During an aircraft accident in which four Ebens were killed, our Team witnessed a ritual, or 'funeral', whereby the Eben bodies were wrapped in a white cloth, various liquids were poured over the bodies while a large group of Ebens stood in a circle chanting.

Serpo Time

One of the greatest dilemmas that our Team faced during their journey dealt with time. On Serpo, time was different. They were never quite able to figure it out. Ebens had no clocks and they found our accounting of time to be unusual. All the Team Members brought wrist watches and other types of timepieces with them, but they no long had a reference. The days on Serpo were longer and a 24 hour clock had no relevance in this star system.

After about 2 years, the Team became confused with the calendar since they weren't able to accurately keep track of the days. The problem was magnified when some of the batteries on the battery-operated timepieces died. With such confusion in time, they discarded their working timepieces and stopped keeping track. The 10 year mission was stretched into 13 years.

One complication that arose due to the differences in how time was kept dealt with physics. In nearly all physics calculations the requirement of time as a variable is used. Our Team had to come up with an alternate method to measure speeds, and orbits. Even with some of the best military scientists, simple problems involving Kepler's Law of Planetary Motion couldn t be calculated in the conventional way. Our scientists ultimately determined that Kepler s Law, as it applies on Earth, did not apply to that solar system.

Trying to explain our science to an alien civilization who didn't know Einstein or Maxwell, and had no notion of the concept of minutes, hours, days, months, years, turned into quite a challenge.

Serpo Inventory List

TESTING EQUIPMENT:

IOO pieces of geological testing items
2 military soil-testing stations
2 chemistry-testing stations (civilian)
6 radiation-testing meters
2 military radiation-testing stations
2 biological testing stations (civilian)
2 IOOcc tractors
4 IOOcc digging tool tractors
IO pre-packed military Soil Testing Kits
I6 astronomical telescopes
2 Military Star Stations
4 military power generators
4 civilian power generators
Experimental solar collecting equipment
50 portable two-way FM radios
6 military combat radio platform kits
50 pre-packed military radio repair kits
I,000 different frequency tubes
30 electrical testing and repair kits
3 solar testing stations (military)
I experimental solar testing station
IO solar collection panels
IO air sample collection kits (military)
5 air sample collection kits (civilian)
6 diamond drills
IO military special access kits
I,000 pounds of C-4 explosives
500 blasting caps
Detonating cord and Time fuse
Military shape charges
I Nuclear Detonating Kit

VEHICLES:

IO military-style combat motorcycles
3 military M-I5I Jeeps
3 military trailers
IO Military repair kits for jeeps
IO Military repair kits for the motorcycles
I Military lawn mower
I,500 gallons of fuel

FOOD:

C-Rations
25 pre-packed containers
I00 containers of freeze-dried food items
I00 cases of various canned food items
7 years worth of vitamins
I00 containers of energy bars/snack items
I,000 gallons of water
I50 military survival food kits
I6 boxes of various alcoholic wines
I50 cases of drinking fluids
Chewing gum, lifesaver candy and misc food items

CLOTHING:

24 pairs of specialized flight suits
II2 pairs of underwear (pants/shirts)
220 pairs of socks
I8 hats (jungle style and regular ball caps)
50 different types of footwear
Military load bearing belts and harnesses
Military backpacks
30 pairs of civilian casual pants
Shorts
Sleeveless shirts
I5 pairs of athletic shoes
I00 pairs of athletic socks
8 athletic supports
24 pairs of thermal underwear
24 pairs of thermal socks
6 pairs of cold weather boots
Military-style hot weather clothing
60 pairs of gloves military work-style
I0 containers of military-style sanitary gloves
6 pairs of cold weather gloves
I0 laundry bags
Disposal surgical gloves
Military-style warm weather jackets
Military-style cold weather jackets
Civilian-style warm and cold weather jackets
I0 pairs of warm weather sandals
24 military safety helmets
24 military-style flight helmets
I,000 yards of fabric

MEDICAL EQUIPMENT:

Portable X-ray machine
100 pre-packed, battlefield medical kits
Examination scopes
Eye examination equipment
120 pre-packed surgical kits
120 pre-packed medicine kits
30 military-style medical sanitation kits
75 water testing kits (military style)
50 water testing kits (civilian)
75 FAST kits
1,200 food-testing kits
500 pieces of misc. surgical tools
5,000 packages of insect repellant
250 medical intravenous kits/with fluids
16 pre-packed medical testing kits
50 pre-packed medical testing kits (civilian)
5 military Medical Portable Hospital Tents
2 Military Medical Portable Deployment Kits
18 Military Medical Blood testing kits
3 portable military chemistry stations
2 Advanced Biological Testing Kits
15 Military Radiation Treatment Kits
1,000 pounds of misc. medical equipment

MUSIC:

Pop/Contemporary:
Elvis Presley
Buddy Holly
Ricky Nelson
The Kingston Trio
Brenda Lee
The Beach Boys
Bob Dylan
Peter Paul & Mary
The Beatles
Loretta Lynn
Simon & Garfunkel
The Hollies
Chubby Checker
Bing Crosby
Dinah Shore
Vera Lynn
Tommy Dorsey
Ted Lewis
Ethel Merman
Everly Brothers
Lesley Gore
Marline Dietrich
The Platters
Doris Day
Connie Francis
Shirelles Lyrics
Frank Sinatra
Dean Martin
Perry Como
Guy Lombardo
Glenn Miller
Rosemary Clooney
Al Jolson

Classical Music:
Mozart
Handel
Bach
Schubert
Mendelssohn
Rossini
Strauss
Beethoven
Brahms
Chopin
Tchaikovsky
Vivaldi

Other:
Christmas Music
US Patriotic Music
Indian Chanting
Tibetan Chants
African Chants

MISCELLANEOUS EQUIPMENT and ITEMS:

IOO military blankets & IOO military sheets
24 military combat deployment kits
80 pre-packed military combat tent kits
4 military mobile kitchen deployable kits
6 military survival stations warm weather
6 military survival stations cold weather
2 military weather stations combat style
50 military weather balloons
24 military handguns
24 military rifles (M-I6s)
6 M-66 weapons
2 M-40 grenade launchers
2 military 60mm motor tube (30 rounds)
IOO military air burst flares
5,000 rounds of .223 ammunition
500 rounds of .45 ammunition
60 M-40 rounds
I5 Freon dispersal containers
I5 compressed air dispersal containers
20 tanks of oxygen gas
20 tanks of nitrogen gas
20 tanks of gases for cutting equipment
75 military-style sleeping bags
60 military-style pillows
55 military-style sleeping platforms
6 military combat living platforms
250 different style padlocks
6,000 feet of different types of rope
24 repelling kits
IO seismic deep hole drills
I,000 gallons of fuel
4 military-style phonographs
IO Military cassette players
IO reel-to-reel tape players
60 belts
IO military sound collection equipment kits
25 military Intelligence Collection Kits
I,000 other miscellaneous items

PINUPS

1: Jake Ekiss

2: Armando M. Zanker

3: Guy LeMay

4: Mile Williams (pencils)
Jimmy Tournas (inks)
Kris Carter (colors)

5: Ramon Espinoza

eKiss

GUY

MW '08
carter

102
ACADEMICALLY I HAD EVERYTHING
PODDED INTO MY BRAIN
EVEN HAD ME STUDYING SOME
CREATED TO CONFUSE THE
ME TELL YOU... IT WAS
TAUGHT A NUMBER OF
ESPINOZA
APR 2008
WED 02

And now, an exclusive preview of

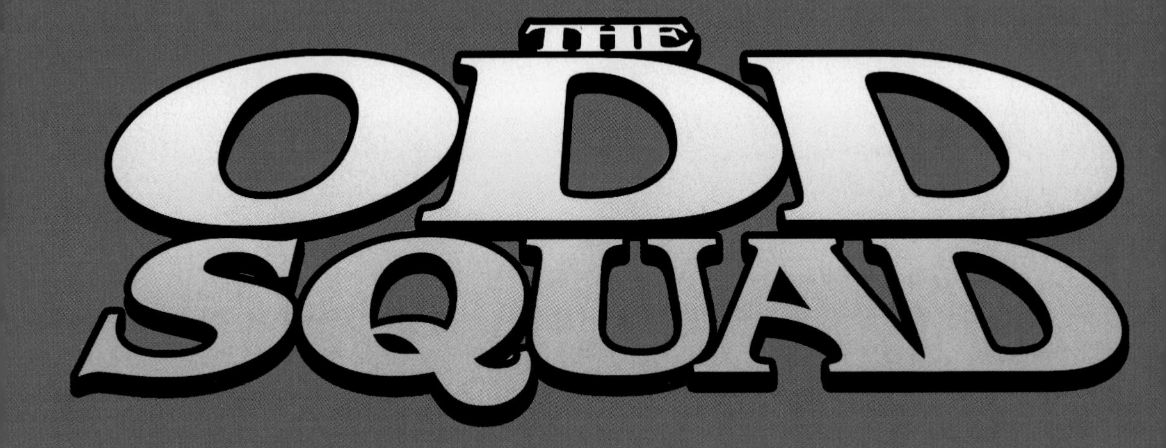

a brand new title
coming Fall 2008
from

THE ODD SQUAD

CROOKED RIVER, OREGON.
SHERIFF! YOU REALLY BETTER GET OUT HERE. WE HAVE A BIT OF A SITUATION.

DAMMIT, TOM!! I GET TEN FLIPPIN' MINUTES A DAY TO MY-SELF!
THE WHOLE REASON I TRAINED YOU AS MY DEPUTY WAS SO YOUR DUMB ASS COULD HANDLE... WHOA.

TOM, YOU HAVE MY APOLOGIES.
OKAY, EASY SON. YOU DON'T WANT TO DO ANYTHING YOU MIGHT REGRET.
OTHER THAN POINTING A WEAPON AT A POLICEMAN?

XACTLY. IF YOU'RE NOT AREFUL, YOU COULD BE OCKED AWAY FOR THE REST OF YOUR LIFE.
HAT'S RECISELY WHAT WANT, SHERIFF.

I ASKED YOUR DEPUTY NICELY TO SECURE ME BEHIND BARS, BUT HE DIDN'T TAKE ME SERIOUSLY, SO I HAD TO RESORT TO MORE DRASTIC MEASURES.
WHY WOULD ANYONE **WANT** TO BE PUT IN JAIL?

AT NIGHT, I TURN INTO A WILD ANIMAL. I TRANSFORM! AND DO ... WHO KNOWS WHAT!? I DON'T REMEMBER IN THE MORNING. I CAN'T BE TRUSTED! AND IT'S ALMOST DARK NOW! THAT'S WHY YOU NEED TO **LOCK ME UP!!**
OKAY, OKAY.

TOM, CALL THE WHITE HOUSE.
TELL THEM WE HAVE THE PRESIDENT'S SON IN THE COOLER.

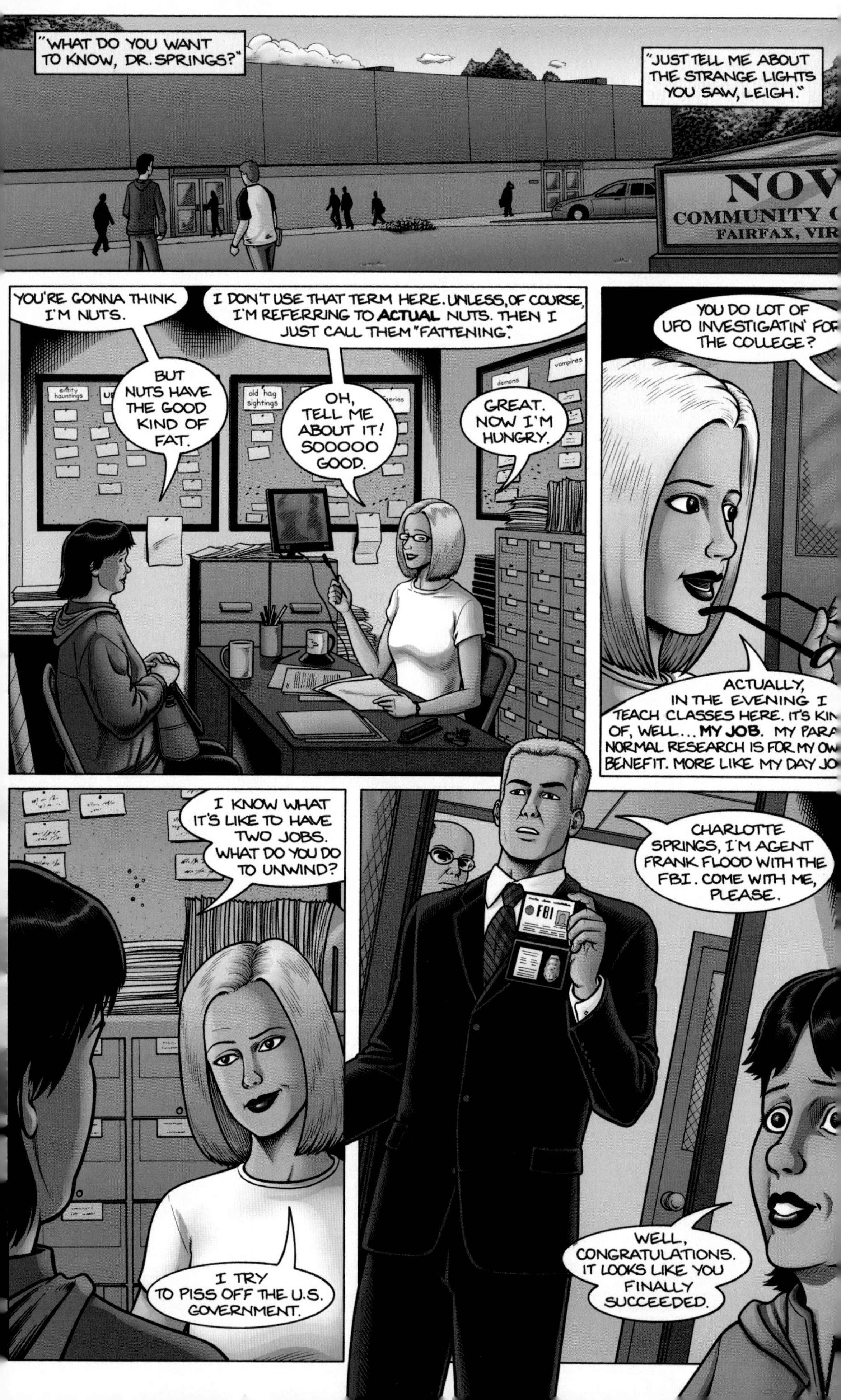
"WHAT DO YOU WANT TO KNOW, DR. SPRINGS?"
"JUST TELL ME ABOUT THE STRANGE LIGHTS YOU SAW, LEIGH."
NOV
COMMUNITY C
FAIRFAX, VIR
YOU'RE GONNA THINK I'M NUTS.
I DON'T USE THAT TERM HERE. UNLESS, OF COURSE, I'M REFERRING TO ACTUAL NUTS. THEN I JUST CALL THEM "FATTENING."
BUT NUTS HAVE THE GOOD KIND OF FAT.
OH, TELL ME ABOUT IT! SOOOOO GOOD.
GREAT. NOW I'M HUNGRY.
entity hauntings
old hag sightings
demons
vampires
YOU DO LOT OF UFO INVESTIGATIN' FOR THE COLLEGE?
ACTUALLY, IN THE EVENING I TEACH CLASSES HERE. IT'S KIN OF, WELL... MY JOB. MY PARA NORMAL RESEARCH IS FOR MY OW BENEFIT. MORE LIKE MY DAY JO
I KNOW WHAT IT'S LIKE TO HAVE TWO JOBS. WHAT DO YOU DO TO UNWIND?
I TRY TO PISS OFF THE U.S. GOVERNMENT.
CHARLOTTE SPRINGS, I'M AGENT FRANK FLOOD WITH THE FBI. COME WITH ME, PLEASE.
FBI
WELL, CONGRATULATIONS. IT LOOKS LIKE YOU FINALLY SUCCEEDED.

ISN'T IT GREAT THAT WE FINALLY GET TOGETHER FACE-TO-FACE, FRANK FLOOD?
I WORK IN WASHINGTON, DC, MA'AM. I GET TO MEET CRAZY PEOPLE EVERY DAY.

S JUST THAT AFTER ALL THE "CEASE ND DESIST" LETTERS RUBBER AMPED WITH YOUR SIGNATURE, FEEL LIKE WE'RE OLD FRIENDS.
DON'T TOUCH ME, PLEASE.

OH MY GOD, I JUST TOTALLY HAD A PROM FLASHBACK. MY PROM DATE WAS GAY. STILL IS, I GUESS -- I HAVEN'T SEEN HIM SINCE HIGH SCHOOL. HEY, CAN YOU USE YOUR CONTACTS TO CHECK ON THAT FOR ME?
I'D PREFER IT IF YOU DIDN'T TALK TO ME EITHER.

LIKE YOUR NAME: FRANK FLOOD. IT'S VERY ALLITERATIVE A NATURAL DISASTER KIND OF WAY. OH, PLEASE TELL E YOU WORK WITH ERNIE EARTHQUAKE AND TOMMY TORNADO! LET ME GUESS -- YOUR PARTNER HERE IS MICHAEL MUDSLIDE?
YOU'RE STILL TALKING TO ME.

NO HANDCUFFS? AREN'T YOU AFRAID I'M GOING TO ESCAPE?
YOU'RE NOT UNDER ARREST.
SO, THIS ISN'T ABOUT MY FREEDOM OF INFORMATION DEMANDS FOR DOCU-MENTS ON THE PARANORMAL AND EXTRA-TERRESTRIAL INCIDENTS I'VE INVESTIGATED?
OH-- IT IS.

I'VE BEEN ORDERED TO TAKE YOU TO THE CHIEF OF STAFF.
HE'S NOT A GHOST OR AN ALIEN OR ANYTHING, BUT TRY TO GIVE HIM YOUR FULL ATTENTION ANYWAY.

GOOD MORNING, I'M GORDON BECK.
HI, I'M--
CHARLOTTE SPRINGS, 29 YEARS OLD, ORPHANED AT AGE SIX, ONE YOUNGER SISTER-- SEPARATED AFTER YOUR PARENT'S DEATH, FOSTER PARENTS MISSING, PRESUMED DEAD-- SINGLE, NEVER MARRIED, NO CHILDREN...
WAIT-- IS THIS AN EPISODE OF "THIS IS YOUR DEPRESSING LIFE?"

DOCTORATE IN PARAPSYCHOLOGY FROM THE UNIVERSITY OF EDINBURG
YOU'RE WELL RESPECTED IN THE COMMUNITY OF GHOST HUNTERS, PSYCHICS AND UFO HUNTERS.
WHICH MEANS YOU'RE NOT WELL RESPECTED IN MOST OTHER COMMUNITIES.
Y'KNO YOU HAV ALL TH CHARM OF A NIPPLE CLAM

DR. SPRINGS, MY JOB AS CHIEF OF STAFF IS TO MAKE SURE PRESIDENT STERLING'S PEOPLE WORK AS A TEAM.
UNTIL NOW, THEY HAVE.

THE PRESIDENT HAS A... PERSONAL MATTER THAT IS AFFECTING HIS POLITICAL DECISIONS. HE HAS ASKED ME TO OFFER YOU A JOB, WHICH, FOR YOUR OWN GOOD AND THE GOOD OF THE COUNTRY, I WANT YOU TO TURN DOWN.

THOUGH WE ALL APPRECIATED YOUR FATHER'S ERVICE AS THE HEAD OF O.D.D., YOUR NAUTHORIZED CONTINUATION HIS WORK IS BOTH ILL-VISED AND ILLEGAL.
LARS WASN'T MY FATHER.
BUT WE WANT TO BE FAIR. YOU'VE COMMITTED...
TWENTY-EIGHT.
...TWENTY-EIGHT INDICTABLE OFFENSES WE ARE WILLING TO FORGET IF YOU PLAY BALL.
CHARLOTTE SPRINGS!
MR. PRESIDENT!
SORRY, GORDON!
I HEARD YOU WERE HERE, CHARLOTTE! JUST WANTED TO WELCOME YOU ABOARD AND SAY THANKS FOR HELPING!
UH...

YOU KNOW AGENT FLOOD HERE?
OH, WE'RE BFFs, SIR.
EXCELLENT. HE'S A GOOD MAN.
HE'S GOING TO BE WORKING UNDER YOU, BUT HE'S PROBABLY ALREADY TOLD YOU THAT. ANYTHING YOU NEED -- ASK GORDON!

WELL, GORDON, I GUESS I'LL TAKE THE JOB. WHAT IS IT?
THE PRESIDENT HAS REINSTATED THE O.D.D. AND...
AND WANTS TO PUT YOU IN CHARGE.
To Be Continued In The Odd Squad #1!

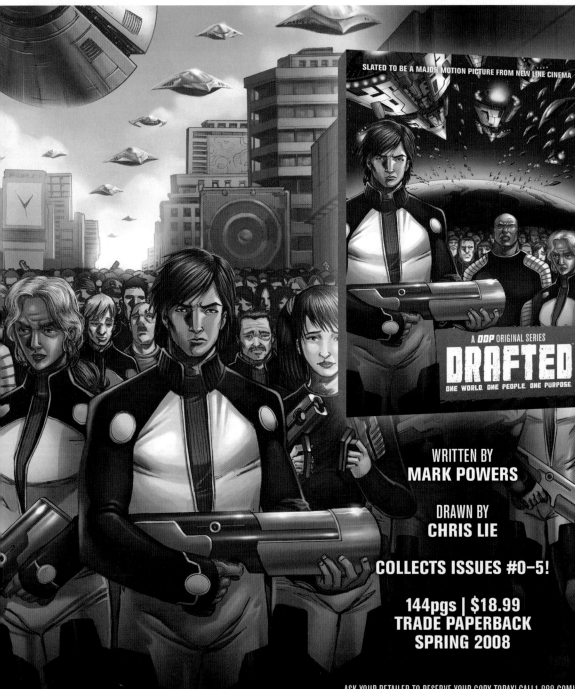

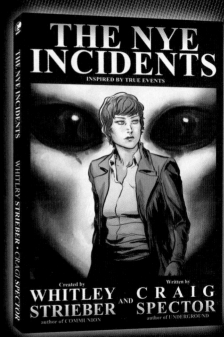